Guy de Maupas
Born in 1850, G
story. In his brief li
four volumes of stories   most of his life
By the time of his death   1893 he had written over 340 sto....s.

Anthony Guise, himself an exponent of the short story, and
extensively published in Britain and abroad, read history at Oxford
and is a literary prize-winner. He lives in London.

On Horseback and Other Stories

On Horseback and Other Stories

Guy de Maupassant

SELECTION BY EDMUND HOWARD

FOREWORD BY ANTHONY GUISE

CAPUCHIN CLASSICS

CAPUCHIN CLASSICS
LONDON

These stories were first published at various dates
between 1877 and 1891
This edition published by Capuchin Classics 2008

© Capuchin Classics 2008

Capuchin Classics
128 Kensington Church Street, London W8 4BH
Tel: +44 (0)207 221 7166
Fax: +44 (0)207 792 9288
E-mail info@capuchin-classics.co.uk
www.capuchin.classics.co.uk

Châtelaine of Capuchin Classics: Emma Howard
Translation editor: Anthony Guise

ISBN-13: 978-0-9555196-9-7

CONTENTS

Foreword   5

On Horseback   7

Madame Tellier's Establishment   15

Mademoiselle Fifi   42

The Necklace   55

The Piece of String   64

That Pig of a Morin   72

The Horla   84

Two Little Soldiers   112

The Christening   119

FOREWORD

Guy de Maupassant (1850-93) wrote some 340 stories, at a headlong rate following his eruption on the literary scene in France in 1880 with the publication of virtually the first of them, the famous *Boule de Suif.* The following nine years were immensely productive, and included two novels and many articles. He wrote for the money and geared the stories and their subject matter to the varied journals he offered them to; and they were high and low. Yet he was an unerring craftsman and his eye for the required detail, his unflinching and pitiless, yet never moralizing, account of the human condition, and his sense of form, never deserted him. He was, and is, a master of the genre. Flaubert, conveniently a childhood friend of his mama, had guided him; Zola championed him. Fame ensued on the instant; he was handsome, urbane and sought after, yet he barriered himself against intrusion into his privacies, even to this very day. He remained close to this mother, whom his father left when he was 13. Known-of lovers notwithstanding, he never married.

Edmund Howard's selection for Capuchin exemplifies these gifts and the range of his themes; and the stories reveal fragments of his life. *On Horseback* (*A Cheval*) surely draws upon some figure of his own acquaintance during his early employment in the civil service, following the sudden impoverishment of his by no means undistinguished family, where the descendant of long-faded aristocracy working for a pittance in the Ministry of Drudge is grotesquely penalized for his pretensions as a chevalier. As a womaniser in his wild oats days, de Maupassant was surely no stranger to such a bordello as *Madame Tellier's Establishment*, exquisitely peopled and narrated with exactly the apt Chekhovian inconsequentiality of plot. Guy himself had briefly been in uniform, aged 20, during the brutish assault by Prussia of France in 1870: a humiliation which cut the future writer to the quick. Yet in *Mademoiselle Fifi*, whose characters are re-created with wicked precision, de Maupassant is not merely engaged in revenge but – characteristically – in choosing his heroine from life's gutter. The touch of genius in *The Necklace* is surely in the unexpected inner response of the female protagonist to the consequences of her self-induced if utterly forgivable catastrophe. As for *The Piece of String*, we recall that the de Maupassants were a Norman family and could risk satirising their own kind in terms not dissimilar to the slant the English give to Scottish compatriots. Wretched, luckless Morin – *That Pig of a Morin* – to be thus exposed to the ruthlessness of the reputation he so indelibly, yet pathetically, indeed virtually innocently, earned for himself!

Darker hues crowd in upon the last three of this collection. *The Horla* is one of de Maupassant's very last stories, dating from some three years before the end, when the syphilis he contracted, most probably in early life (notwithstanding his unawareness of its invasion of him), had begun to besiege him with paranoia. The last two of our collection tell of that other constituent of the French nation Guy knew so well, the Bretons: poignantly so – *desperately* poignantly – in *The Two Little Soldiers*, and no less than savagely so in *The Christening*. The jaw drops.

Anthony Guise
London, 2008

ON HORSEBACK

T he household survived on the meagre income derived from the husband's insignificant appointments. Two children had been born of the marriage and the family's lack of means had developed into a condition of quiet, concealed, shamefaced misery, the poverty of a noble family, which, in spite of misfortune, never forgets its rank.

Hector de Gribelin had been educated in the country, under the paternal roof, by an aged priest. His people were not rich, but they managed to get by and keep up appearances. When Hector reached twenty years of age, they tried to find him a position, and he entered the Ministry of Marine as a clerk at sixty pounds a year. He foundered on the rock of life like all those who have not been prepared for its hard struggles, who look at life through a mist, who do not know how to look out for themselves, whose special aptitudes and natural gifts have not been developed from childhood, whose early training has not developed the rough energy needed for the battle of life or furnished them with tool or weapon. His first three years of office work were a martyrdom.

He had, however, renewed the acquaintance of a few friends of his family – elderly people, far behind the times, and poor like himself, who lived in the right part of Town, the gloomy thoroughfares of the Faubourg Saint-Germain; and he had created a social circle for himself.

Strangers to modern life, humble yet proud, these needy aristocrats lived in the upper stories of sleepy, old-world houses. From top to bottom of their dwellings the tenants were titled, but money seemed just as scarce on the ground floor as on the top.

Their eternal prejudices, absorption with rank, anxiety lest they should lose caste, filled the minds and thoughts of these families once so brilliant, now ruined by the inaction of the men of the family. Hector de Gribelin met in this circle a young girl as well born and as poor as himself and married her. They had two children in four years.

For four years more the husband and wife, harassed by poverty, knew no other distraction than the Sunday walk in the Champs-Elysées and a few evenings at the theatre (amounting in all to one or two in the course of the winter) which they owed to free passes presented by one friend or another.

But in the spring of the following year some overtime work was entrusted to Hector de Gribelin by his superior for which he received the significant sum of three hundred francs.

The day he brought the money home he said to his wife:

'My dear Henrietta, we really ought to do something with this windfall, an outing for the children, say.'

And after a long discussion it was decided that they should go and have a picnic in the country. 'Just once will not break us,' declared Hector. 'So we'll hire a carriage for you, the children and the maid. And I'll hire a horse; the exercise will do me good.'

The whole week long they talked of nothing but the projected excursion. Every evening, on his return from the office, Hector caught up his elder son, put him astride his leg, and, making him bounce up and down as hard as he could, said: 'That's how daddy will gallop next Sunday.'

And the lad amused himself all day long bestriding chairs, dragging them around the room and shouting: 'This is daddy on horseback!'

The servant herself gazed at her master with awestruck eyes as she thought of him riding alongside the carriage, and at meal-times she listened with all ears while he spoke of riding and recounted the exploits of his youth when he lived at home with his father. Oh, he had learned in a good school, and once he felt his steed between his legs he feared nothing – nothing whatever!

Rubbing his hands, he repeated gaily to his wife: 'If only they could give me a feisty animal, I'd be all the better pleased. You'll see how well I can ride; and if you like, we'll come back by the Champs-Elysées just as all the people are returning from the Bois. As we shall cut a pretty good figure, I shouldn't at all object to meeting someone from the ministry. That is all one needs to ensure the respect of one's bosses.'

On the appointed day the carriage and the riding horse arrived at the same moment before the door. Hector went down immediately to examine his mount. He had had straps sewn to his trousers and flourished in his hand a whip he had bought the previous evening. He lifted the horse's legs and felt them one after another, passed his hand over the animal's neck, flank and hocks, opened its mouth, examined its teeth, declared its age; and then, the whole household having collected around him, he delivered a discourse on the horse in general and the specimen before him in particular, pronouncing the latter excellent in every respect.

When the rest of the party had taken their seats in the carriage he examined the girth; then, putting his foot in the stirrup, he sprang into the saddle. The animal began to curvet and nearly threw its rider.

Hector, not altogether at his ease, tried to soothe it.

'Come along old fellow. Gently now!'

When the horse had recovered its equanimity and the rider his nerve, the latter asked: 'Are you ready?' The occupants of the carriage replied with one voice that they were. 'Forward!' he commanded. And the cavalcade set out.

All eyes were upon him. He trotted in the English style, rising unnecessarily high in the saddle; looking at times as if he were mounting into space. Sometimes he seemed on the point of falling forward onto the horse's mane. His eyes were fixed, his face drawn, his cheeks pale. His wife, holding one of the children on her knees, and the servant, who was carrying the other, continually cried out: 'Look at papa! Look at papa!' And the two boys, intoxicated by the motion of the carriage, by their delight and by the fresh air, uttered shrill cries.

The horse, frightened by the noise, started off at a gallop, and while Hector was trying to control his steed his hat fell off. The driver had to get down and pick it up. When the equestrian had recovered it he called to his wife from a distance: 'Don't let the children scream like that! They'll make the horse bolt.'

They lunched on the grass in the Vesinet woods, having brought food with them in the carriage. Although the driver was looking after the three horses, Hector rose every few minutes to see if his own lacked anything. He patted it on the neck and fed it on bread, cake and sugar. 'He's a great trotter,' he declared. 'He certainly shook me up a bit at first, but, as you saw, I soon had him under control. He knows his master now and won't give any more trouble.'

As had been decided, they returned by way of the Champs-Elysées. That spacious thoroughfare literally swarmed with vehicles of every kind, and on the pavements the pedestrians were so numerous that they looked like two long black ribbons unfurling their length from the Arc de Triomphe to the Place de la Concorde. A flood of sunlight played on this cheerful scene, making the varnish of the carriages, the steel of the harness and the handles of the carriage doors shine with dazzling brilliancy. A ferment of life and motion seemed to have invaded this assemblage of people, carriages and horses. In the distance, the outlines of the Obelisk could be discerned in a cloud of golden mist.

As soon as Hector's horse had passed the Arc de Triomphe it became suddenly imbued with fresh energy. Realising that its stable was not far off it began to trot rapidly through the maze of wheels despite all his rider's efforts to restrain him. The carriage was now far behind. When the horse arrived opposite the Palais de l'Industrie, it saw a clear field ahead, and, turning to the right, set off at a gallop.

An old woman in an apron was crossing the road in leisurely fashion. She happened to be just in Hector's way as he arrived on the scene at full speed. Powerless to control his mount, he shouted at the top of his voice: 'Hey! Look out there! Hey!'

She must have been deaf, for she continued blandly on her way until the awful moment when, struck by the horse's chest as by a locomotive under full steam, she turned three somersaults and ended up ten feet away. Several people were yelling: 'Stop him!'

Frantic with alarm, Hector clung to the horse's mane shouting: 'Help! Help!'

A terrible jolt hurled him, as if shot from a gun, over his horse's ears and cast him into the arms of a policeman who was running up to stop him. In the space of seconds, a furious, gesticulating, vociferating group had gathered around him. An old gentleman with a white moustache, wearing a large round decoration, seemed particularly incensed. 'Confound it!' he was declaring. 'When a fellow's as awkward as all that he should remain at home and not come killing people in the streets, and if he doesn't know how to handle a horse, he should stay at home.'

Four men arrived on the scene, carrying the old woman. She appeared to be dead. Her skin was like parchment, her bonnet on one side and she was covered with dust.

'Take her to a chemist's,' ordered the old gentleman, 'and let us go to the commissary of police.'

Hector started on his way with a policeman on either side of him and a third leading his horse, a crowd following. At that moment, the carriage appeared. His wife, grasping what had happened at a glance, jumped down in consternation; the servant lost her head; the children whimpered. Hector explained that he would soon be at home, that he had knocked a woman down and that there was not much the matter.

And his distracted family went on their way.

When they arrived at the police station, the explanation was given in few words. He gave his name – Hector de Gribelin, employed at the Ministry of Marine: and they awaited news of the injured woman. A constable who had been sent to obtain information returned, saying that she had recovered consciousness, but was complaining of frightful internal pain. She was a charwoman, sixty-five years of age, named Madame Simon.

When he heard that she was not dead, Hector's spirits rose and he promised to defray her doctor's bill. Then he hastened to the chemist's. The doorway was thronged; huddled in an armchair, the injured woman was groaning pitifully. Her arms hung at her sides, her face was drawn. Two doctors were still engaged in examining her. No bones were broken, but they feared some internal lesion. Hector addressed her:

'Are you hurting a lot?'

'Oh yes!'

'Where is the pain?'

'I feel as if my insides are on fire.'

A doctor approached. 'Are you the gentleman who caused the accident?'

'I am.'

'This woman ought to be sent to a nursing home. I know one where they would take her at six francs a day. Would you like me to send her there?'

Hector was delighted at the idea, thanked him and returned home much relieved. He found his wife awaiting him in tears. He reassured her. 'It's all right. This Madame Simon is better already and will be quite well in two or three days. I have sent her to a home. It's all right.'

When he left his office the next day he went to inquire for Madame Simon. He found her eating rich soup with an air of satisfaction.

'Well?' said he.

'Oh sir,' she replied. 'I'm just the same. I feel sort of crushed – not a bit better.'

The doctor declared they must wait and see; some complication or other might arise. Hector waited three days, then returned. The old woman, fresh-faced and clear-eyed, began to whine when she saw him:

'I can't move sir; I can't move a bit. I shall be like this for the rest of my days.'

A shudder ran through Hector. He asked for the doctor, who merely shrugged his shoulders and said: 'What can I do?' I can't tell what's wrong with her. She shrieks when they try to raise her. They can't even move her chair from one place to another without her uttering the most distressing cries. I am bound to believe what she tells me; I can't look into her inside. So long as I have no chance of seeing her walk, I've no right to suppose she's shamming.'

The old woman listened, motionless, a malicious gleam in her eyes.

A week passed, then a fortnight, then a month. Madame Simon did not leave her armchair. She ate from morning to night, grew fat, chatted gaily with the other patients and seemed to enjoy her immobility as if it were the rest to which she was entitled after fifty years of going up and down stairs, of turning mattresses, of carrying coal from one floor to another, of sweeping and dusting.

Hector, at his wit's end, came to see her every day. Every day he found her calm and serene and constantly declaring: 'I can't move sir. I shall never be able to move again.'

Every evening, Madame de Gribelin worn with anxiety, said: 'How is Madame Simon?'

And every time he replied with a resignation born of despair: 'Exactly the same; no change whatever.'

They dismissed the servant, whose wages they could no longer afford. They economised more rigidly than ever. The whole of the bonus had been swallowed up. Then Hector summoned four noted doctors, who met in consultation over the old woman. She let them examine her, feel her, sound her, watching them with a cunning eye.

'We must make her walk,' said one.

'But sirs, I can't!' she cried. 'I can't move!'

Then they took hold of her, raised her and dragged her a short distance, but she slipped from their grasp and fell to the floor, groaning and giving vent to such heartrending cries, that they carried her back to her seat with infinite care and precaution.

They reserved their opinion – agreeing, however, that work was an impossibility to her.

When Hector brought his news to his wife she sank on a chair murmuring: 'It would be better to bring her here; it would cost us less.'

He started in amazement. 'Here? In our own house? How can you think of such a thing?'

But she, resigned now to anything, replied with tears in her eyes: 'But what can we do, my love? It's not my fault!'

MADAME TELLIER'S

ESTABLISHMENT

i

They went there every night at about eleven, just as they would go to the club, six or eight of them; always the same set, not fast men, but respectable tradesmen, and young men in the civil service or some other employ. They would drink their Chartreuse and laugh with the girls, or else talk seriously with Madame Tellier, whom everybody respected, then they would go home by midnight! Sometimes the younger men would stay on.

It was a small, comfortable house painted yellow, at the corner of a street behind the church of Saint Etienne. From the windows one could see the docks full of ships being unloaded, the big salt marsh, and, rising beyond it, the Virgin's Hill with its old grey chapel.

Madame Tellier came of a respectable family of peasant proprietors in the Department of the Eure. She had taken up her profession just as if she might have taken up that of a milliner or dressmaker. The prejudice which is so violent and deeply rooted in large towns does not exist in the country places in Normandy. The peasant says: 'It's a paying business', and he sends his daughter off to keep an establishment of this character just as readily as he would send her to keep a girls' school.

She had inherited the establishment from an elderly uncle. Monsieur and Madame Tellier, who had formerly been innkeepers near Yvetot, had promptly sold their house, as they judged the business at Fécamp to be more profitable, and they arrived one fine morning to assume the direction of the enterprise, which was declining suffering from the absence of its owners. They were good people in their way, and were soon on good terms with the neighbours.

Monsieur died of a stroke two years later, for as the new place kept him in idleness and without any exercise, he had grown far too stout, and his health had suffered. Now that Madame was a widow, all the habitués made much of her; but people said that, personally, she was very proper, and even the girls in the house could discover nothing against her. She was tall, full of figure and affable, and her complexion, which had become pale in the gloom of the house, whose shutters were scarcely ever opened, shone as if it had been varnished. She had a fringe of curly false hair, which gave her a youthful look that contrasted sharply with the ripeness of her body. She was always smiling and cheerful and fond of a joke, but there was a shade of reserve about her which her new occupation had not quite made her shed. Coarse words invariably shocked her, and when any young fellow who had been badly brought up called her establishment by its proper name, she was angry and indignant.

In a word, she had a refined mind, and although she treated her women as friends, yet she would frequently comment that 'she and they were not made of the same stuff'.

Sometimes during the week she would hire a carriage and take some of her girls into the country, where they used to enjoy themselves on the grass by the side of the little river. They were like a bunch of girls let out from school for the day, and would run races and play childish games. They had a cold dinner on the grass, and drank cider, and went home at night with a delicious feeling of fatigue; in the carriage they kissed Madame Tellier as if a kind mother, full of goodwill and complaisance.

The house had two entrances. At the corner there was a sort of tap-room, which sailors and the lower orders frequented at night, and she had two girls whose special duty it was to wait on them with the assistance of Frédéric, a short, light-haired, beardless fellow, as strong as a horse. They laid out half bottles of wine and jugs of beer on the shaky marble tables for the customers, and encouraged the men to drink.

The three other girls – there were only five of them – formed a kind of aristocracy; they remained with the clients on the first floor, unless they were needed downstairs and there was nobody on the first floor. The Jupiter drawing room, where the tradesmen used to meet, was papered in blue, and embellished with a large representation of Leda and the swan. The room was reached by a winding staircase through a narrow door opening on the street, and above this door a lantern enclosed in a wire grille, such as one still sees in some towns at the foot of the shrine of some saint, burned all night long.

The house, which was old and damp, had a faint odour of mildew. At times there was a whiff of eau de Cologne in the passages and sometimes from a half-open door downstairs the racous mirth of the common men sitting and drinking rose to the first floor, much to the disapproval of the gentlemen who were there. Madame Tellier, who was on friendly terms with her customers, did not leave the room; she took much interest in what was going on in the town, and they regularly told her all the news. Her serious conversation was a change from the ceaseless chatter of the three women; it was a rest from the obscene jokes of those portly persons who every evening indulged in the commonplace debauchery of drinking a glass of liqueur in company with whores.

The names of the girls on the first floor were Fernande, Raphaële, and Rosa the Jade. As the staff was limited, madame had endeavoured that each member should be an exemplary, an epitome of a feminine type, so that every customer might find as nearly as possible the realization of his ideal.

Fernande represented the handsome blonde: she was very tall, rather fat and lazy, a country girl, who could not get rid of her freckles and whose short, pale, almost colourless hair, like combed-out hemp, barely covered her head.

Raphaële, who came from Marseilles, played the indispensable part of the handsome Jewess, and was thin, with high cheekbones daubed with rouge, and her black hair greased with marrowfat curled around her forehead. Her eyes would have been handsome if the right one had not had a white speck in it. Her beaky nose came down over a square jaw, on which two false upper teeth contrasted strangely with the discolour of the rest.

Rosa was a little ball of fat, nearly all body, with very short legs; from morning till night she sang songs, alternately risqué or sentimental, in a husky voice; told pointless interminable tales, and only stopped talking in order to eat, and stopped eating in order to talk. She was never still, and was active as a squirrel, in spite of her embonpoint and her short legs. Her laugh, which was a torrent of shrill cries, resounded here and there, ceaselessly, in bedroom, attic and café, everywhere, and anywhere, and all about nothing.

The two women on the ground floor were Louise, nicknamed La Cocotte, and Flora, called the Seesaw, because she limped a little. The first always dressed as the Goddess of Liberty, with a tri-coloured sash, and the other as a Spanish woman, with a string of copper coins in her carroty hair, which jingled at every uneven step – both looked like cooks dressed up for the carnival. They were like all other women of the lower orders, neither uglier nor better looking than they usually are.

They looked just like servants at an inn, and were generally called 'the two Beer-Pulls'.

An uneasy peace, very rarely disturbed, reigned among these five women, thanks to Madame Tellier's conciliatory wisdom and her constant good humour. The establishment was the only one of the kind in the little town and was much frequented. Madame Tellier had succeeded in giving it such a respectable appearance, she was so congenial and obliging to everybody, her good nature was so well known, that she was treated with a certain respect. The regular customers spent money on her, and were delighted at any special gesture of friendship from her. When they met during the day, they would say: 'Until this evening, you know where', just as men say: 'At the club, after dinner.' In a word, Madame Tellier's house was somewhere to go to, and they very rarely missed their daily meetings there.

One evening towards the end of May, the first arrival, Monsieur Poulin, a timber merchant, who had been mayor, found the door shut. The lantern behind the grating was not alight; there was not a sound in the house; everything seemed dead. He knocked, gently at first, then more loudly, but nobody answered the door. Then he went slowly up the street, and when he got to the market place he met Monsieur Duvert, the gun-maker, on his way to the same place; so they went back together, but met with no better success. Suddenly they heard a loud noise, close to them, and on going round the house, they saw a number of English and French sailors, who were hammering at the closed shutters of the tap-room with their fists.

The two good townsmen immediately made their escape, but a low 'Pst!' stopped them: it was Monsieur Tournevau, the fish-curer, who had recognized them, and was trying to attract their attention. They told him what had happened, and he was all the more put out, he being a married man and father of a family, who only went on Saturdays. That was his regular evening. Now he would be deprived of this dissipation for the whole week.

The three men went as far as the quay together, and on the way they met young Monsieur Philippe, the banker's son, who frequented the place regularly, and Monsieur Pinipesse, the tax collector. They all returned to the Rue aux Juifs together, to make a last attempt. But the frustrated sailors were besieging the house, throwing stones at the shutters, and shouting. The five first-floor customers withdrew as smoothly as possible, and walked aimlessly about the streets.

Presently they met Monsieur Dupuis, the insurance agent, and then Monsieur Vasse, the Judge of the Tribunal of Commerce, and they took a long walk, going first to the pier. Here they sat down in a row on the granite parapet and watched the rising tide. After they had been there for some time, Monsieur Tournevau said: 'This is not at all amusing!'

'It certainly isn't,' Monsieur Pinipesse replied, and they set off to walk away again.

Taking the street called Sous-le-Bois, they returned by the wooden bridge which crosses the Retenue, and passed close to the railway. On coming out again on the market-place, suddenly, a quarrel flared between Monsieur Pinipesse the collector and Monsieur Tournevau about an edible mushroom which one of them declared he had found in the neighbourhood.

As they were already out of temper from having nothing to do, they would very probably have come to blows if the others had not interfered. Monsieur Pinipesse went off furious, and soon another altercation arose between the ex-mayor, Monsieur Poulin, and Monsieur Dupuis, the insurance agent, on the subject of the tax collector's salary and the profits which he might make. Insulting remarks were passing freely between them, when a torrent of formidable cries was heard, and the body of sailors, fed up with waiting so long outside a closed house, came into the square. They were walking arm in arm, two and two, forming a long procession, and were bawling at the top of their voices. The townsmen hid in a doorway, and the yelling crew disappeared in the direction of the abbey. For quite some time they still heard the noise, which diminished like a storm in the distance; then silence was restored. Monsieur Poulin and Monsieur Dupuis, furious with each other, went in different directions without wishing each other goodbye.

The other four set off again, and instinctively went in the direction of Madame Tellier's establishment, which was still closed, silent and impenetrable. A quiet but obstinate drunken man was knocking at the door of the lower room, and then stopped and called Frédéric in a low voice. Finding that he got no answer, he sat down on the doorstep and waited for what would happen next.

The others were just going to retire, when the rowdy bunch of sailors reappeared at the end of the street. The French sailors were bawling out the 'Marseillaise', and the Englishmen 'Rule Britannia'. There was a general lurching against the wall, and then on they went on their way towards the quay, where a fight broke out between the two nations, in the course of which an Englishman had his arm broken and a Frenchman his nose split.

By this time the drunken man who had waited outside the door was whimpering, as drunken men and children whimper when vexed, and the others went away. By degrees calm was restored in the riotus town; here and there, at moments, the far-off sound of voices could be heard, then died away in the distance.

One man only was still wandering about, Monsieur Tournevau, the fish-curer, miserable at the thought of having to wait until the following Saturday. He hoped something would turn up, he did not know what. He was exasperated at the police for thus allowing an establishment of such public utility, which they had under their aegis, to be closed.

He went back to it and examined the walls, trying to find out some reason, and on the shutter he saw a notice stuck up. He struck a wax match and read the following, in a large, uneven hand: 'Closed for First Communion'.

Then he went away, seeing it was useless to remain, and leaving the drunk lying on the pavement fast asleep outside that inhospitable door.

Next day all the regular customers, one after the other, found one reason or another for going along the street, bundles of papers under their arms to keep them in countenance, and with a furtive glance they all read that mysterious notice:

'Closed for First Communion.'

ii

Madame Tellier had a brother who was a carpenter in their native place, Virville, in the Department of Eure. When she still kept the inn at Yvetot, she had stood godmother to that brother's daughter, who had received the name of Constance – Constance Rivet; Madame herself being a Rivet on her father's side. The carpenter, who knew that his sister was well set up, did not lose sight of her although they did not meet often since both were kept at home by their occupations, and lived some distance from each other. But now the girl was twelve and going to be making her First Communion, he seized the opportunity to write to his sister, asking her to come and be present at the ceremony. Their old parents were dead; she could hardly refuse and accepted the invitation. Her brother, whose name was Joseph, hoped that by dint of giving his sister attention, she might be induced to make her will in the girl's favour, since she had no children of her own.

His sister's occupation did not trouble his scruples in the least, and, besides, nobody knew anything about it at Virville. When they spoke of her, they only said: 'Madame Tellier is living at Fécamp', which might mean that she was living on her own private income. It was a good fifty miles from Fécamp to Virville, and for a peasant fifty miles on land is as long a journey as crossing the ocean would be for city people. The inhabitants of Virville had never been farther than Rouen, and nothing attracted the people from Fécamp to a village of five hundred houses in the middle of a plain and situated in another department. Anyway, nobody knew anything about her business.

But the Communion was approaching, and Madame Tellier was in considerable embarrassment. She had no deputy, and did not at all care to leave her house even for a day. All the rivalries between the girls upstairs and those downstairs would infallibly break out. No doubt Frédéric would get drunk, and when he was in that state, he would knock anybody down on a whim. At last, however, she made up her mind to take them all with her, except for the man, to whom she gave a holiday until the next day but one.

When she asked her brother, he made no objection, and undertook to put them all up for a night. So, on Saturday morning, the eight o'clock express carried off Madame Tellier and her companions in a second-class carriage. As far as Beuzeville they were alone, and chattered like magpies, but at that station a couple got in. The man, an old peasant, dressed in a blue blouse with a turned-down collar, wide sleeves tight at the wrist, ornamented with white embroidery, in an old high hat with long nap, held an enormous green umbrella in one hand and in the other a large basket from which the heads of three frightened ducks protruded. The woman, who sat stiffly erect in her rustic finery, had a face like a hen, with a nose as pointed as a beak. She sat down opposite her husband and did not stir, somewhat alarmed at finding herself in such smart company.

There was certainly an array of striking colours in the carriage. Madame Tellier was dressed in blue silk from head to foot, and had on a dazzling red imitation French cashmere shawl. Fernande was struggline for breath in a Scotch plaid dress, whose bodice her companions had laced as tight as they could, forcing up her full bust. Raphaële's bonnet was festooned with feathers so that it looked like a bird's nest. She had on a lilac dress with gold spots on it, and there was something Oriental about it that suited her Jewish face. Rosa wore a pink skirt with large flounces, and looked like a very fat child, an obese dwarf; while the Two Beer-pulls looked as if they had cut their dresses out of old flowered curtains dating from the Restoration.

As soon as they were no longer alone in the compartment, the ladies put on staid looks, and began to talk of subjects which might give others a high opinion of them. But at Bolbec a gentleman with light whiskers, a gold chain, and wearing two or three rings, got in, and put several parcels wrapped in oilcloth on the rack over his head. He was evidently a good-hearted fellow and perhaps something of a wag.

'Are you ladies changing your quarters?' he enquired, and that question caught them off balance. Madame Tellier, however, quickly regained her composure, and said sharply, to avenge the honour of her corps:

'I think you might try to be polite!'

He excused himself, and said: 'I beg your pardon, I ought to have said your nunnery.'

She could not think of a retort, so, perhaps thinking she had said enough, Madame gave him a dignified bow and pursed her lips.

Then the gentleman, seated between Rosa and the old peasant, began to wink knowingly at the ducks whose heads were sticking out of the basket. When he felt that he had caught the attention of his public, he began to tickle them under the bills and spoke facetiously to them to make the company smile.

'We have left our little pond, quack! quack! to make the acquaintance with a little spittle, qu-ack! qu-ack!'

The unfortunate creatures twisted their heads away, to avoid his fingerese, making desperate efforts to escape their wicker prison, then suddenly, all at once, uttered the most lamentable squawks of distress. The women exploded with laughter. They leaned forward and jostled each other, so as to see better; they were thoroughly interested in the ducks, and the gentleman redoubled his antics, wit and chaff.

Rosa joined in, and leaning over her neighbour's legs, she kissed the three animals on the head, and immediately all the girls wanted to kiss them in turn. As they did so the gentleman took each onto his knee, bounced them up and down and pinched their arms. The two peasants, in greater consternation even than their poultry, rolled their eyes as if possessed, not venturing to move. Their old wrinkled faces had not so much as a smile, not a twitch.

Then the gentleman, a commercial traveller, offered the ladies suspenders by way of a joke, and taking up one of his packages, he opened it. It was a joke, for the parcel contained garters. There were blue silk, pink silk, red silk, violet silk, mauve silk garters, and the buckles were made of two gilt metal cupids embracing each other. The girls uttered exclamations of delight and looked at them with that gravity natural to all women when they are considering an article of dress. They consulted one another by their looks or in a whisper, and replied in the same manner, and Madame Tellier was longingly handling a pair of orange garters that were broader and more imposing-looking than the rest; really fit for the mistress of an establishment such as hers.

The gentleman was biding his time, for he had an idea.

'Come, my dears,' he said, 'you must try them on.'

There was a torrent of exclamations, and they squeezed their petticoats between their legs, but he quietly bided his time and said: 'Well, if you won't try them on I shall pack them up again.' And he added slyly: 'I'm offering any lady who tries them on to have this pair for nothing.'

But they simply would not, sitting very straight and looking haughty.

But the two Beer-pulls looked so distressed that he renewed his offer. Flora, especially, visibly hesitated, and he insisted: 'Come, my dear, a little courage! Just look at that lilac pair; it will go with your dress perfectly.'

That decided her, and pulling up her dress she showed a thick leg fit for a milkmaid, in a badly fitting, coarse stocking. The commercial traveller stooped down and fastened the garter. When he had done this, he gave her the lilac pair and asked: 'Who next?'

'Me! Me!' they all shouted at once. He began on Rosa, who uncovered a shapeless, round thing without any ankle, a regular 'sausage of a leg' as Raphaële used to say.

Lastly, Madame Tellier herself put out her leg, a handsome, muscular

Norman leg, and in his surprise and pleasure, the commercial traveller gallantly took off his hat to salute that master calf, like a true French cavalier.

The two peasants, speechless with astonishment, stealing glances out of the corner of the eye, looked so exactly like chickens that the man with the pale side whiskers, standing up, went: 'Cock-a-doodle-doo', under their very noses, which gave rise to another burst of merriment.

The old couple got out at Motteville with their basket, their ducks and their umbrella, and they heard the woman say to her husband as they moved away: 'They are no-gooders and off to that wicked place, Paris.'

The jokey commercial traveller himself got out at Rouen, after behaving so coarsely that Madame Tellier was obliged sharply to put him in his place, and adding, as a moral: 'This will teach us not to talk to any Tom, Dick or Harry.'

At Oissel they changed trains, and at a little station farther on down the line was Monsieur Joseph Rivet waiting for them with a large cart containing a number of chairs in it, drawn by a white horse.

The carpenter politely kissed all the ladies and then helped them into his conveyance. Three of them sat on three chairs at the back; Raphaële, Madame Tellier and her brother on the three chairs in front; while Rosa, without a seat, settled herself as best she could on tall Fernande's knees. Then off they set.

However the horse's jerky trot shook the cart so violently that the chairs began to dance and tossed the travellers about, right and left, as if they were dancing puppets, which had them squeaking and screwing up their faces. They clung on to the sides of the vehicle, their bonnets falling down on their backs, over their faces and accross their shoulders. The white horse went on stretching his head forward and holding out his little tail which was as hairless as a rat's, with which he whisked his haunches from time to time.

With one leg on the shafts and the other doubled under him, M.

Rivet held the reins with his elbows very high, and kept uttering a kind of clucking sound which made the horse prick its ears and go faster.

The green country stretched out on either side of the road, and here and there the flowering rape presented a waving expanse of yellow. The wind carried its strong, wholesome, sweet odour a long way. Amid the rye the cornflowers showed their little blue heads, and the women wanted to pick them, but M. Rivet refused to stop.

Then, sometimes, so thick were the poppies that a whole field appeared covered with blood; and the cart, which looked as if it were filled with flowers of more brilliant hue, jogged on through fields bright with wild flowers, disappearing behind the trees of a farm only to reappear and to go on again through the yellow or green standing crops, studded with red or blue.

One o'clock struck as they drove up to the carpenter's door. They were tired out and pale with hunger, having eaten nothing since they left home. Madame Rivet ran out and helped them down, one by one, kissing them as soon as they were on the ground, and it seemed she would never tire of kissing her sister-in-law whom she apparently wanted to monopolize. They had lunch in the workshop, which had been cleared for the next day's dinner.

The delicious omelette, followed by boiled chitterlings and washed down with good hard cider, made them all feel in good cheer.

Rivet had taken a glass so that he might drink with them. His wife cooked, waited on them, brought in the dishes, took them out and asked each of them in a whisper whether they had everything they wanted. A number of boards standing against the walls and heaps of shavings swept into the corners gave out the scent of planed wood, the aroma of a carpenter's shop – that resinous odour which penetrates the lungs.

They wanted to see the little girl, but she had gone to church and would not be back again until evening, so they all set out for a stroll in the country.

It was a small village, through which the highroad passed. Ten or a dozen houses on either side of the single street were inhabited by the butcher, the grocer, the carpenter, the innkeeper, the shoemaker and the baker.

The church was at the end of the street and was surrounded by a small graveyard; four immense lime-trees, which stood just outside the porch, overshadowed it entirely. It was built of flint, in no particular style, with a slate-roofed steeple. When you got past it, you were again in the open country, broken here and there by clumps of trees which hid the homesteads.

Rivet had given his arm to his sister, out of politeness, although he was in his working clothes, promenading her with a certain solemnity. His wife, who was overwhelmed by Raphaële's gold-striped dress, walked between her and Fernande. Rosa was trotting behind with Louise and Flora the Seesaw, limping along, now quite tired out.

The villagers came to their doors, the children left off playing, and a curtain would be twitched aside, to reveal a muslin cap, while an old woman with a crutch, almost blind, crossed herself as if it were a religious procession. They all gazed for a long time at these striking ladies from town who had come so far to be present at the First Communion of Joseph Rivet's little girl. The carpenter had surely risen in public estimation.

As they passed the church they heard some children singing. Shrill little voices were singing a hymn, but Madame Tellier would not let them go in for fear of disturbing the little cherubs.

After the walk, during which Joseph Rivet enumerated the principal landed proprietors and spoke about the yield of the land and the productiveness of the cows and sheep, he took his bevy of women home and settled them in. As it was a very small place, they had to put them all up two to a room. Just this once Rivet would sleep in the workshop on the shavings; his wife was to share her bed with her sister-in-law, and Fernande and Raphaële were to sleep together in the next room. Louise and Flora were put into the kitchen, where they had a mattress on the floor, and Rosa had a little dark cupboard to herself at the top of the stairs, next to the garret, where the candidate for First Communion was to sleep.

When the little girl came in she was overwhelmed with kisses; all the ladies wished to caress her, with that instinctive need for tenderness expressed and their habit of professional affection such as had had them kissing the ducks in the railway carriage.

Each took the girl on their knees, stroked her soft, fine hair and squeezed her in their arms with vehement and spontaneous outbursts of affection, and the child, who was very good and religious, bore it all patiently.

As the day had been a fatiguing one for everybody, they all went to bed soon after dinner. The whole village was wrapped in that perfect stillness of the country, which is almost like a religious silence. The girls, who were accustomed to the noisy evenings of Madame Tellier's, were rather affected by the perfect repose of the sleeping village. They shivered, not with cold, but with those little shivers of loneliness which touch uneasy and troubled hearts.

As soon as they were in bed, two and two together, they clasped each other in their arms as if to protect themselves against this feeling of the calm and profound slumber of the earth. But Rosa, alone in her little dark cupboard, felt a vague and painful emotion come over her.

She was tossing about, unable to get to sleep, when she heard the faint sobs of a crying child close to her head, through the partition. She was frightened, and called out, and was answered by a weak voice, broken by sobs. It was the little girl, who was always used to sleeping in her mother's room and was afraid in her tiny garret.

Rosa was delighted, crept out of bed so as not to awaken anyone, and went and fetched the child. She took her into her warm bed, kissed her and pressed her to her bosom, lavished exaggerated manifestations of tenderness on her, and at last grew calmer herself and went to sleep. And till morning the candidate for First Communion slept with her head on

Rosa's bosom.

At five o'clock the little church bell, ringing the Angelus, woke the women, who usually slept the whole morning long.

The villagers were up already, and women went busily from house to house, carefully carrying short, starched muslin dresses or very long wax tapers tied in the middle with a bow of silk fringed with gold, and with dents in the wax for the fingers.

The sun was already high in the blue sky, still with a rosy tint on the horizon like a faint lingering trace of dawn. Families of chickens were pecking around outside the houses, and here and there a black cock, with a glistening breast, raised his head, crowned by his red comb, flapped his wings and uttered his shrill crow which the other cocks repeated.

Vehicles of all sorts came from neighbouring parishes, stopping by at the various houses, and tall Norman women dismounted, wearing dark dresses, kerchiefs crossed over the bosom and fastened with silver brooches a hundred years old. The men had put on their blue smocks over their new frock-coats or over their old dress-coats of green broadcloth, the tails of which hung down below their blouses.

When the horses were in the stables there was a double line of rustic conveyances along the road: carts, cabriolets, tilburies, wagonettes, traps of every shape and age tipping forward on their shafts or else tipping backward with the shafts in the air.

The carpenter's house was as busy as a beehive. The women, in dressing-jackets and petticoats, with their thin, short hair, which looked faded and worn, hanging down their backs, were busy dressing the child, who was standing quietly on a table, while Madame Tellier was directing the movements of her battalion. They washed her, did her hair, dressed her, and with the help of a number of pins, they arranged the folds of her dress and took in the waist which was too loose.

Then, when she was ready, the girl was told to sit down and not to move, and the women hurried off to get ready themselves.

The church bell began ringing again, its tinkle was lost in the air, like a feeble voice underneath wide skies. The candidates came out of the houses and went towards the parochial building, which comprised the two schools and the mansion house and which stood at the opposite end of the village to the church. Parents, in their very best clothes, followed their children, with self-conscious expressions, and those awkward movements of bodies bent by toil.

The little girls disappeared in a cloud of muslin, which looked like whipped cream, while the lads, like embryo waiters in a café and whose heads shone with marrow-fat, walked with their legs apart, so as not to get any dust or dirt on their black trousers.

It was something for a family to be proud of, when a large number of relatives who had come from a distance surrounded the child. The carpenter's triumph was complete. Madame Tellier's regiment, its leader at its head, followed Constance; her father gave his arm to his sister, her mother walked by the side of Raphaële, Fernande with Rose and Louise and Flora together, and thus they proceeded majestically through the village, like a general's staff in full uniform. The effect on the village was startling.

At the school the girls ranged themselves under the Sister of Mercy and the boys under the schoolmaster, and off they set, singing a hymn as they went. The boys led the way in double file between the two rows of carts and traps, from which the horses had been taken out. The girls followed in the same order; and as all the people in the village had given the town ladies precedence out of politeness, they came immediately behind the girls, and lengthened the double line of the procession still more, three on the right and three on the left, while their dresses were as striking as a display of fireworks.

When they entered the church the congregation were dumbfounded. They pressed against each other, twisted round and jostled one another to catch a glimpse, and some of the devout ones spoke almost in raised voices, so astonished were they at the sight of those ladies whose dresses were more elaborate than the priest's vestments.

The mayor offered them his pew, in the front on the right, close to the choir. Madame Tellier sat there with her sister-in-law. Fernande and Raphaële, Rosa, Louise and Flora occupied the second pew, in company with the carpenter.

The choir was full of kneeling children, girls on one side and boys on the other, and the long wax tapers which they held looked like lances pointing in all directions. Three men were standing in front of the lectern, singing as loud as they could. They prolonged the syllables of the sonorous Latin indefinitely, holding on to 'Amens' with interminable '*Aaas*', which the reed stop of the organ sustained in a monotonous, long-drawn-out tone. A child's shrill voice gave the responses. From time to time a priest, sitting in a stall and wearing a biretta, got up, muttered something and sat down again, while the three singers continued, their eyes fixed on the big book of plainchant lying open before them on the outstretched wings of a wooden eagle.

Silence ensued, then the service went on. Towards the close Rosa, with her head in both hands, suddenly thought of her mother, her village church and her First Communion. She almost fancied that that day had returned when she was so small and was almost hidden in her white dress, and she began to cry.

First of all she wept silently, and the tears dropped slowly from her eyes, but her emotion swelled with her recollections, and she began to heave with sobs. She took out her pocket handkerchief, wiped her eyes and held it to her mouth to stifle her cries, but it was in vain. A sort of rattle escaped her throat, and she was answered by two other profound, heartbreaking sobs, for her two neighbours, Louise and Flora, who were kneeling near her, overcome by similar recollections, were sobbing by her side, amid a flood of tears, Since tears are contagious, Madame Tellier soon in turn found that her eyes were wet,

32

and on turning to her sister-in-law, she saw that all the occupants of her pew were also weeping.

Soon, throughout the church, here and there, a wife, a mother, a sister, seized by the strange sympathy of poignant emotion, and affected at the sight of those handsome ladies on their knees shaken with sobs, was moistening her cambric pocket handkerchief and pressing her beating heart with her left hand.

Just as the sparks from an engine will set fire to dry grass, so the tears of Rosa and of her companions infected the whole congregation in a moment. Men, women, old men and lads in new smocks were soon all sobbing. Something superhuman seemed to be suspending over their heads a spirit, the powerful breath of an invisible and all-powerful Being.

Suddenly a species of madness seemed to pervade the church – the noise of a congregation in a state of frenzy, a tempest of sobs and stifled cries. It came like gusts of wind which blow the trees in a forest. The priest, paralysed by emotion, stammered out incoherent prayers, without finding words, ardent prayers of the soul soaring to Heaven.

The people behind him gradually grew calmer. The cantors, in all the dignity of their white surplices, went on in somewhat uncertain voices, and the reed stop itself seemed hoarse, as if the instrument had been weeping. The priest, however, raised his hand to command silence and went and stood on the chancel steps, when everybody fell immediately silent.

After a few remarks on what had just taken place, which he attributed to a miracle, he continued, turning to the seats where the carpenter's guests were sitting:

'I especially thank you, my dear sisters, who have come from such a distance, and whose presence among us, whose evident faith and ardent piety, have set such a salutary example to all. You have edified my parish; your emotion has warmed all hearts; without you, this great day would not, perhaps, have had this truly divine character. It is sufficient, at times, that there should be one chosen lamb, for the Lord to descend amid His flock.'

His voice faltered, and he concluded: 'May the grace of God be with you.'

'Amen!'

They now left the church as quickly as possible; the children themselves were restless and tired out after such an emotional tension. The parents slipped away to see about the meal.

There was a crowd outside, quite a hubbub of loud voices with the sing-song Norman accent distantly audible. The villagers formed two ranks, and when the children appeared, each family took possession of its own.

The whole houseful of ladies caught hold of Constance, surrounding her and kissing her, and Rosa especially demonstrative. Finally taking hold of one hand, while Madame Tellier took the other. Raphaële and Fernande held up her long muslin skirt, to prevent it trailing in the dust; Louise and Flora brought up the rear with Madame Rivet. The child herself, very silent and thoughtful, set off for home in the midst of this guard of honour.

Dinner was served in the workshop on long boards supported by trestles.Through the open door they could see all the merry-making that was going on in the village. Everywhere they were feasting. Through every window were to be seen tables surrounded by folk in their Sunday best, and a cheerful noise was heard in every house. The men sat in their shirt-sleeves, downing glass after glass of cider.

In the carpenter's house the gaiety was relatively subdued from all the emotion of the girls in the morning; Rivet was the only one who was in a festive mood, and he was boozing hard. Madame Tellier glanced at the clock repeatedly since if two days running were not to be lost they must catch the 3.55 train, which would bring them to Fécamp by nightfall.

The carpenter tried very hard to divert her attention so as to keep his guests until the next day, but he did not succeed, for she never took things lightly when it came to business. As soon as they had had their coffee she ordered her girls to buck up and get ready. Turning to her brother, she said: 'You must put in the horse right away', and she herself went upstairs to finish her preparations to be off.

When she came down again, her sister-in-law was waiting to speak to her about the child, and a long conversation took place in which, however, nothing was settled. The carpenter's wife was artful and made a considerable show of affection, and Madame Tellier, propping the girl on her knee, would not commit herself to anything definite, but merely made vague promises – she would not forget her, there was plenty of time, and besides, they would meet again.

Meanwhile, no cart had come to the door and the ladies did not come downstairs. Upstairs they even heard loud laughter, scuttling and squeaking and much clapping of hands. While the carpenter's wife went to the stable to see if the cart was ready, madame went upstairs.

Rivet, who was very drunk, was plaguing Rosa, who was half choking with laughter. Louise and Flora were holding him by the arms and trying to calm him, shocked at his levity after the morning's ceremony; but Raphaële and Fernande were goading him on, convulsed with laughter and holding their sides, uttering shrill cries at every rebuff the drunken fellow received.

Rivet was red in the face, and trying to shake off the two women who were clinging to him, while he was dragging at Rosa's skirt with all his might and protesting 'So you won't, you slut, won't you?'

Madame Tellier, very indignant, went up to her brother, seized him by the shoulders, and threw him out of the room with such violence that he fell against the wall in the passage. A minute afterward they heard him pumping water on his head in the yard, and when he reappeared with the cart he had sobered up entirely.

They took the same route they had come by the day before, and the little white horse started off with his quick, dancing trot. Under the hot sun, hilarity, checked during the dinner, broke out again. The girls now were amused at the jolting of the cart, pushed their neighbours' chairs and burst out laughing at the least provocation.

There was a shimmering haze across the fields which dazzled their eyes, and the wheels raised two trails of dust along the road. Presently, Fernande, who was fond of music, asked Rosa to sing something, and she boldly struck up the 'Fat Curé of Meudon', but Madame Tellier made her stop immediately, since she considered it a most unsuitable song for such a day. 'Sing us something of Béranger's,' she said. After a moment's hesitation, Rosa indeed began Beranger's song 'The Grandmother' in her husky voice, and all the girls, and even Madame Tellier herself, joined in the chorus:

> *Combien je regrette*
> *Mon bras si dodu,*
> *Ma jambe bien faite,*
> *Et le temps perdu!*

'That's the stuff,' Rivet declared, carried away by the rhythm, and they bawled out the refrain to every verse, while Rivet beat time on the shaft with his foot and with the reins on the back of the horse, which – as if he himself were carried away by the rhythm – broke into a wild gallop, and threw all the women in a heap on top of the one another, on the floor of the cart.

They got up, roaring with laughter, and on went the song, shouted at the top of their voices, beneath the burning sky, among the ripening grain, as the little horse sped along, breaking into a gallop each time the refrain was sung, every hundred yards or so, to their great delight. The occasional stone-breaker by the roadside sat up and gazed at the cartload of shouting females through wire spectacles.

When they got out at the station, the carpenter said: 'I am sorry you are going. We might have had some good times together.'

Madame Tellier replied most correctly: 'Everything has its right time, and we cannot always be enjoying ourselves.'

And then Rivet had a sudden inspiration: 'Look here, I will come and see you at Fécamp next month,' and gave Rosa a roguish look.

'You may come if you like', his sister replied, 'but you are not to be up to any of your tricks.'

He did not reply, and as they heard the whistle of the train, he immediately began to kiss them all. When it came to Rosa's turn, he tried to get to her mouth which she, however, smiling with her lips closed, twisted away from him each time by a rapid movement of her head to one side. He clutched her in his arms, but could not attain his object, as his large whip, which he was holding in his hand and waving behind the girl's back in desperation, impeded his movements.

'Passengers for Rouen, take your seats!' the guard cried, and in they got. There was a whistle from the guard, followed by a loud whistle from the engine which noisily puffed forth its first jet of steam, while the wheels began to turn with visible effort. Rivet, leaving the platform, ran along by the track to get another glimpse of Rosa; and as the carriage passed him he began to crack his whip and to hop, while he sang at the top of his voice:

> *Combien je regrette*
> *Mon bras si dodu,*
> *Ma jambe bien faite,*
> *Et le temps perdu!*

He watched a white pocket-handkerchief which somebody was waving as the train disappeared in the distance.

iii

They slept the sound sleep of a quiet conscience, until they got to Rouen, and when they returned to the house, refreshed and rested, Madame Tellier could not help remarking: 'It was all very well, but I'm glad to be home.'

They hurried over their supper, and then, when they had put on their usual evening costume, settled down to wait for their regular customers. The little coloured lamp outside the door told the passers-by that Madame Tellier had returned, and in a flash the news got round, nobody knew how or through whom.

Monsieur Philippe, the banker's son, even carried friendliness so far as to send a special messenger to Monsieur Tournevau, in the bosom of his family. The fish-curer had several cousins to dinner every Sunday, and they were having coffee when a man came in with a letter in his hand. Monsieur Tournevau, much excited, opened the envelope and turned pale; it contained just these words in pencil:

The cargo of cod has been located; the ship has come into port; good business for you. Come at once.

He felt in his pockets, slipped the messenger two sous, and suddenly blushing to his ears, he said: 'I have to go out.' He handed his wife the laconic and mysterious note, rang the bell, and when the servant came in, asked her to bring him his hat and overcoat immediately. As soon as he was in the street, he began to hurry, and the distance seemed to him to be twice as long as usual, so impatient was he. Madame Tellier's establishment had put on quite a holiday look. On the ground floor, a number of sailors were making a deafening noise. Louise and Flora were drinking first with one then the other, and were being called for in every direction at once. The upstairs room was in full swing by nine o'clock. Monsieur Vasse, the Judge of the Tribunal of Commerce, Madame Tellier's regular but Platonic wooer, was conversing with her in a corner in a low voice, and both were smiling as if they were about to come to an understanding.

Monsieur Poulin, the ex-mayor, had Rosa astride him, with her pressing her nose against his and her fat little hands running through the old gentleman's white side whiskers. She had hitched up her yellow skirt for a patch of white thigh to show against the dark cloth of his trousers, and her red stockings were held up by the blue garter the commercial traveller had given her.

Tall Fernande was on the sofa, with her feet on the tummy of Monsieur Pinipesse the tax collector, and propped against young Monsieur Philippe, with her right arm around his neck and a cigarette in her left hand.

Raphaële appeared to be in serious consultation with Monsieur Dupuis, the insurance agent, which she was concluding: 'Yes, my darling, this evening,' and piroutted accross the room calling out: 'Tonight, it's all okay!'

Just then the door flew open and Monsieur Tournevau came in, to be greeted with enthusiastic cries of 'Good old Tournevau!' And Raphaële, still dancing around the room, threw herself into his arms. He seized her in a vigorous embrace and, without saying a word, lifted her up as if she had been a feather, crossed the drawing-room with her and disappeared through the door at the end, leading to the staircase up to the bedrooms to the accompaniment of applause.

Rosa was doing her best to amuse the ex-mayor, kissing him and pulling both his whiskers simultaneously, to keep his head straight.

'Come along,' she told him. 'Monsieur Tournevau has set us an example'; and the dear old boy followed Rosa out of the room.

Fernande and Madame Tellier remained with the four men, and Monsieur Philippe exclaimed: 'I'll pay for champagne; do bring three bottles, Madame Tellier.' Fernande gave him a hug, and whispered: 'Play us a waltz, will you?' So up he got and, sat down at the old piano in the corner, and managed to coax a tinny waltz out of the depths of the instrument.

The tall girl put her arms round the tax collector. Madame Tellier let Monsieur Vasse take her round the waist, and the two couples turned round, kissing as they danced. Monsieur Vasse, who had formerly danced in society, waltzed with such elegance that Madame Tellier was quite captivated, regarding him with a look that said 'Yes' more eloquently than any spoken word.

Frédéric brought the champagne; the first cork popped, and Monsieur Philippe played the opening of a quadrille, which the four dancers took in society fashion, decorously, with propriety, deportment, bows and curtsies. Then they began to drink.

Monsieur Philippe next struck up a lively polka, and Monsieur Tournevau, who had returned, started off with the handsome Jewess whom he held without letting her feet touch the ground. Monsieur Pinipesse and Monsieur Vasse had started off with renewed vigour, and from time to time one or other couple would throw down a long draught of sparkling wine. The dance was threatening to become never-ending when Rosa, handsome in a nightdress and candle in hand, opened the door.

'I want to dance,' she declared.

'What about your old boy?' asked Raphaële

'Him?' laughed Rosa. 'He's asleep already. He drops off just like that.' She caught hold of Monsieur Dupuis, idle on the couch, and the dance began again.

But the bottles were empty. 'I'll pay for one,' Monsieur Tournevau said. 'So will I,' Monsieur Vasse declared. 'And I'll do the same,' Monsieur Dupuis came in.

They all began to clap, and it soon became a regular ball. From time to time Louise and Flora nipped upstairs and their customers downstairs grew impatient, when it was discovered that one of the men was missing too.

'And just where have you been?' Monsieur Philippe asked mischievously when Monsieur Pinipesse came back into the room with Fernande.

'Gazing upon Monsieur Poulin sleeping,' replied the tax collector.'

The witticism was a big success, and all the gentlemen in turn went upstairs 'to gaze upon Monsieur Poulin sleeping', together with one or other of the young ladies who were wonderously accommodating that night. Madame turned a blind eye to what was going on. She had a number of private exchanges with Monsieur Vasse, as if she were tying up the final details of a deal which had already been decided between them.

At one o'clock, the two married men, Monsieur Tournaveau and Monsieur Pinipesse finally declared that they must be getting home and asked for their bills. Only the champagne was charged for and at a mere six francs a bottle instead of the usual ten. When they expressed astonishment at this generosity, Madame replied with a beaming smile, 'It's not every day we've something to celebrate.'

MADEMOISELLE FIFI

Major Count von Farlsberg, the Prussian commandant, lay back in a great easy-chair reading his newspaper with his booted feet on the beautiful marble mantelpiece where his spurs had made two holes. These had grown deeper every day during the three months that he had been in the château of Uville.

A cup of coffee was steaming on a small inlaid table, which was stained with liquids, charred by cigar ends, and notched by the penknife of the victorious officer, who would occasionally pause while sharpening a pencil to jot down figures or to make a drawing on its surface, as he felt inclined.

Having read his letters and the German newspapers his orderly had brought him, he got up, and threw three or four enormous green logs on the fire, for these gentlemen were gradually cutting down all the trees in the park to keep themselves warm. He crossed to the window. The rain was coming down in torrents, a regular Normandy rain, which seemed as if it were being poured out by some furious person, a slanting rain, opaque as a curtain, forming a kind of wall with diagonal stripes, and deluging everything, a rain such as one frequently experiences in the neighbourhood of Rouen, which is the piss-pot of France.

For a long time the officer looked at the sodden turf and at the swollen Andelle beyond it, overflowing its banks. He was drumming a waltz with his fingers on the window-panes when a noise made him turn round. It was his second-in-command, Captain Baron von Kelweinstein.

The major was a giant, with broad shoulders and a long, fan-like beard which covered his chest. His whole impressive personage gave one the notion of a military peacock, a peacock with his tail spread out accross his breast. He had cold, gentle blue eyes, and a scar from a sword-cut received in the war with Austria; he was said to be an honourable man, as well as a gallant officer.

The captain, a short, red-faced man, was tightly belted in at the waist, his red hair cropped quite close to his head. In certain lights he looked almost as if he had been rubbed over with phosphorus. He had lost two front teeth one night – he could not quite remember how – and this sometimes made him speak unintelligibly. The bald patch on the top of his head was surrounded by a fringe of curly, bright golden hair, making him look like a monk.

The commandant shook hands and drank his cup of coffee (the sixth that morning), while he listened to his subordinate's report of what had occurred. Then they both went to the window and declared that it was a very unpleasant outlook. The major, a quiet man, with a wife at home, could accommodate himself to everything; but the captain, who was in the habit of frequenting low resorts and enjoyed women's society, was furious at having to be shut up for three months in the compulsory chastity of that wretched hole.

There was a knock at the door. When the commandant said 'Come in' one of the orderlies appeared, announcing by his mere presence that lunch was ready. In the dining-room they met three other officers of lower rank – a lieutenant, Otto von Grossling, and two ensigns, Fritz Scheuneberg and the Marquis von Eyrick, a very short, fair-haired man, proud and brutal towards his men, harsh towards prisoners, and explosive as gunpowder.

Since he had been in France his comrades had called him nothing but Mademoiselle Fifi. They had given him that nickname on account of his dandified style and small waist, which looked as if he wore corsets, of his pale face on which his budding moustache scarcely showed, and on account of the habit he had acquired of employing the French expression, *Fi, fi donc*, which he pronounced with a slight whistle when he wished to express his supreme contempt for persons or things.

The dining-room of the château was a long and magnificent room, whose fine old mirrors, cracked by pistol bullets, and Flemish tapestry, cut to ribbons and hanging in rags in places from sword-cuts, told too well what Mademoiselle Fifi's occupation was during his spare time.

There were three family portraits on the walls: a steel-clad knight, a cardinal and a judge, each of whom was smoking a long porcelain pipe, inserted into holes in the canvas, while a lady with a tight-laced bodice proudly exhibited a pair of enormous moustaches, drawn with charcoal. The officers ate their lunch almost in silence in that mutilated room, which looked drab in the rain and melancholy in its dilapidated condition, although its old oak floor had become as solid as the stone floor of an inn.

When they had finished eating and were smoking and drinking they began, as usual, to grumble at the boring life they were leading. The bottles of brandy and of liqueur passed from hand to hand, and all sat back in their chairs and took repeated sips from their glasses, scarcely removing from their mouths the long, curved stems, which terminated in china bowls painted in a manner that might have pleased a Hottentot.

As soon as their glasses were empty they refilled them with a gesture of resigned weariness, but Mademoiselle Fifi emptied his every minute, and a soldier immediately gave him another. They were enveloped in a cloud of dense tobacco smoke, and seemed sunk in a state of drowsy, stupified intoxication – that condition of stupified intoxication of men who have nothing to do – when suddenly the baron sat up and said: 'Heavens alive! This cannot go on. We must think of something to do.'

And on hearing this, Lieutenant Otto and Ensign Fritz, who pre-eminently possessed the serious, heavy German countenance, said: 'What, captain?'

He thought for a few moments and then replied: 'What? Why, we must get up some entertainment, if the commandant will allow us.'

'What sort of an entertainment, captain?' the major asked, taking his pipe out of his mouth.

'I will arrange all that, commandant,' the baron replied. 'I will send Le Devoir to Rouen, and he will bring back some ladies. I know where they can be found. We'll have supper here. All we need is at hand, and at the very least we shall have a jolly evening.'

Count von Farlsberg shrugged his shoulders and said with a smile: 'You must be mad, my friend.'

But all the other officers had risen and surrounded their chief, saying: 'Let the captain have his way, commandant. It's terribly dull here.' And the major ended by giving way.

'Very well', he replied, and the baron immediately sent for Le Devoir. He was an old non-commissioned officer, who had never been seen to smile, but who carried out all the orders of his superiors to the letter, no matter what they might be. He stood there with an impassive face while he received the baron's instructions, and then went out; five minutes later a large military wagon, covered with tarpaulin, galloped off as fast as four horses could draw it in the pouring rain. The officers all seemed to awaken from their lethargy, their looks brightened, and they began to chatter.

Although it was raining as hard as ever, the major declared that it was not so dark, and Lieutenant von Grossling said with conviction that the sky was clearing, while Mademoiselle Fifi did not seem to be able to keep still. He got up and sat down again, and his bright eyes seemed to be looking for something to destroy. Suddenly, looking at the lady with the moustaches, the young fellow pulled out his revolver and said: 'You shall not see it.' And without leaving his chair he aimed, and with two successive bullets cut out both the eyes of the portrait.

'Let us make a mine!' he then exclaimed, and the conversation was suddenly interrupted, as if they had found some fresh and powerful subject of interest. The mine was his invention, his method of destruction, and his favourite amusement.

When he left the château, the lawful owner, Comte Fernand d'Amoys d'Uville, had not had time to carry away or to hide anything except the plate, which had been stowed away in a hole made in one of the walls. As he was very rich and had good taste, the large drawing-room, which opened into the dining-room, and before his precipitate flight, looked like a gallery in a museum.

Valuable oil paintings, watercolours and drawings hung from the walls, while on the tables, on the hanging shelves and in elegant glass cupboards there were a thousand ornaments: small vases, statuettes, clusters of Dresden china and intricate Chinese figures, old ivory and Venetian glass, which filled the large room with their costly and fantastic array.

Scarcely anything was left now; not that the things had been stolen, for the major would not have allowed that, but Mademoiselle Fifi would every now and then have a mine, and on those occasions all the officers thoroughly enjoyed themselves for five minutes. The little marquis went into the drawing-room to get what he wanted, and returned with a small, delicate china teapot, which he filled with gunpowder. He then carefully pushed a fuse through the spout. This he lighted and took his infernal machine into the next room, after which he came back immediately and shut the door. The Germans stood expectant, their faces full of childish, smiling curiosity, and as soon as the explosion had shaken the château, they all rushed in.

First in was Mademoiselle Fifi, who clapped his hands in delight at the sight of a terracotta Venus, whose head had been blown off, and each picked up pieces of porcelain and wondered at the curious shape of the fragments, while the major was looking with a paternal eye at the large drawing-room, which had been wrecked after the fashion of a Nero and strewn with the fragments of works of art. He went out first and said with a smile: 'That was a great success this time.'

But there was such a cloud of smoke in the dining-room, mingled with the tobacco smoke, that they could not breathe, so the commandant opened the window, and all the officers, who had returned for a last glass of cognac, went up to it.

The moist air blew into the room, bringing with it a sort of powdery spray, which sprinkled their beards. They looked at the tall trees dripping with rain, at the broad valley covered with mist, and at the church spire in the distance, which rose up like a grey point in the driving rain.

The bells had not rung since their arrival. That was the only resistance which the invaders had met with in the neighbourhood. The parish priest had not refused to provide lodging and food for the Prussian soldiers; he had several times even drunk a bottle of beer or claret with the enemy commandant, who often employed him as a benevolent intermediary; but it was no use asking him to ring the bells; he would sooner have allowed himself to be shot. That was his way of protesting against the invasion, a peaceful and silent protest, the only one, he said, suitable to a priest, who was a man of mildness, and not of blood. Everybody, for twenty-five miles round, praised Abbé Chantavoine's firmness and heroism in venturing to proclaim the public mourning by the obstinate silence of his church bells.

The whole village, stirred by his resistance, was ready to back up their pastor and to risk anything, since they looked upon that silent protest as the safeguard of the national honour. It seemed to the peasants that they had set a greater example to their country than Belfort or Strasbourg and that the name of their little village would thus become immortalized; however, with that exception, they refused their Prussian conquerors nothing.

The commandant and his officers laughed among themselves at this inoffensive courage, and as the people in the whole country round showed themselves obliging and compliant towards them, they willingly tolerated their silent patriotism. Little Wilhelm alone would have liked to have forced them to ring the bells. He was very angry at his superior's politic acceptance of the priest's scruples, and every day begged the commandant to allow him to sound 'ding-dong, ding-dong', just once, only just once, just by way of a joke. He asked it in the coaxing, tender voice of some loved woman who is bent on obtaining her wish, but the commandant would not yield, and to console himself, Mademoiselle Fifi made a mine in the Château d'Uville.

The five men stood there together for five minutes, breathing in the damp air, and at last Lieutenant Fritz said with a laugh: 'The ladies will certainly not have fine weather for their drive.' Then they separated, each to his duty, while the captain had plenty to do arranging for the dinner.

When they met again towards evening they began to laugh at the sight of each other as spick and span and smart as on the day of a grand review. The commandant's hair did not look so grey as it was in the morning, and the captain had shaved, leaving only his moustache, which made him look as if he had a streak of fire under his nose.

In spite of the rain, they left the window open, and one of them went to listen from time to time; and at a quarter past six the baron said he heard a rumbling in the distance. They all hurried down, and presently the wagon drove up at a gallop with its four horses steaming and blowing, and splashed with mud to their girths. Five women dismounted, five handsome girls whom a comrade of the captain to whom Le Devoir had presented his card had selected with care.

They had not required much pressing, as they had got to know the Prussians in the three months during which they had had to go along with them, and had resigned themselves to the men as they had to the state of affairs.

They went at once into the dining-room, which looked still more dismal in its dilapidated condition now it was lit up; while the table covered with choice dishes, the beautiful china and glass, and the plate, which had been found in the hole in the wall where its owner had hidden it, gave it the appearance of a bandits' inn, where they were supping after committing a robbery. The captain was radiant, and put his arm round the women as if he were familiar with them. When the three young men wanted to appropriate one each, he opposed them authoritatively, reserving to himself the right to apportion them justly, according to their various ranks, so as not to offend the hierarchy. Therefore, to avoid all argument, invidiousness, and suspicion of partiality, he placed them all in a row according to height, and addressing the tallest, said in a voice of command: 'What is your name?'

'Pamela', she replied, raising her voice. Then he said: 'Number One, called Pamela, is assigned to the commandant.'

Then, having kissed Blondina, the second, as a sign of proprietorship, he proffered stout Amanda to Lieutenant Otto; Eva, 'the Tomato', to Sub-lieutenant Fritz, and Rachel, the shortest of them all, a very young, dark girl, with eyes as black as ink, a Jewess, whose nose obeyed the rule which allots hooked noses to all her race, to the youngest officer, the Marquis Wilhelm von Eyrick.

They were all plump and pretty, without any distinguishing features, and each had a similarity of complexion and style in the light of their daily lovemaking in their communal house.

The three young men wished to carry off their prizes immediately under the pretext that they might wish to powder their noses; but the captain wisely opposed this, insisting they were quite fit to sit down to dinner. His experience in such matters carried the day, so there were only many kisses, expectant kisses.

Suddenly Rachel choked, and began to cough until the tears came into her eyes, while smoke emerged from her nostrils. Under the pretence of kissing her, the marquis had blown a whiff of tobacco into her mouth. She did not fly into a rage, nor even utter a word, but she looked at her tormentor with latent hatred in her dark eyes.

They sat down to dinner: The commandant seemed delighted. He made Pamela sit on his right and Blondina on his left, and said, as he unfolded his table napkin: 'This was a delightful idea of yours, captain.'

Lieutenants Otto and Fritz, who were as polite as if they had been with ladies of society, somewhat intimidated their guests, but Baron von Kelweinstein beamed, made obscene remarks and seemed on fire with his coronet of red hair. He paid the women compliments in Rhineland French and sputtered out gallant remarks, albeit only fit for a pothouse, from between his two broken teeth and amid a battery of spittle.

They did not understand him, however, and their intellects seemed unaroused until he uttered foul words and lurid expressions, mangled by his accent. Then they all began to laugh at once like crazy women and fell against each other, repeating the words, which the baron now purposely mispronounced to give him the pleasure of hearing them utter obscenities. They gave him as much as he wanted, for they were drunk after the first bottle of wine, and resuming their usual habits and manners, they kissed the officers to right and left of them, pinched their arms, uttered wild cries, drank out of every glass and sang French ditties and fragments of German songs which they had picked up in their daily intercourse with the enemy.

Soon the men themselves, worked up by female flesh under their noses and in immediate reach, became quite unrestrained, shouted and broke the plates and dishes, while the soldiers standing behind waited on them impassively. The commandant was the only one who kept himself under control.

Mademoiselle Fifi had taken Rachel on his knee and, getting excited, at one moment kissed the little black curls on her neck and at another pinched her furiously, making her shriek, since he was seized by a species of ferocity, and goaded by his desire to hurt her. He often held her close to him and pressed a long kiss on the Jewess's rosy mouth until she lost her breath, and finally he bit her until a stream of blood ran down her chin and on to her corsage.

For the second time she looked him full in the face, and as she wiped away the blood, she said: 'You will have to pay for that!' But he merely laughed and retorted: 'I will pay.'

At the arrival of dessert, champagne was served, and the commandant rose, and in the same voice in which he would have proposed the health of the Empress Augusta, he drank: 'To our ladies!' And a series of toasts began, toasts worthy of the lowest soldiers and of drunkards, mingled-with obscene jokes which their ignorance of the language made more vicious still. Each got up, one after the other, trying to say something witty, forcing themselves to be funny, and the women, so drunk that they all but fell off their chairs, applauded madly each time.

The captain, who no doubt wished to impart an appearance of gallantry to the orgy, raised his glass again and said: 'To our victories over hearts!' And, thereupon, Lieutenant Otto, who was a species of bear from the Black Forest, jumped up, inflamed with drink, and suddenly seized by an access of alcoholic patriotism, he cried: 'To our victories over France!'

Drunk as they were, the women were silent, except Rachel who turned round, trembling, and said: 'I know some Frenchmen in whose presence you would not dare say that.' But the little marquis, still holding her on his knee, began to laugh, since the wine had made him very hilarious, and said: 'Ha! ha! ha! I've never met any of them myself. As soon as we show ourselves, away they run !' The girl, at the end of her tether, shouted into his face: 'You lie, you sod!'

For a moment he looked at her steadily with his bright eyes upon her, as he had looked at the portrait before he destroyed it with bullets from his revolver, and then he began to laugh. 'Ah yes! Talk about them, my dear! Would we be here now if they were brave?' And, getting worked-up, he exclaimed: 'We are the masters! France belongs to us!' In one bound from his knee she threw herself into her chair while he stood, held forth his glass over the table and repeated; 'France and the French, the woods, the fields and the houses of France belong to us!'

The others, quite drunk, and suddenly seized by military enthusiasm – the enthusiasm of brutes – seized their glasses, and shouting, 'Long live Prussia!' they emptied them at a draught.

The girls did not protest, for they were reduced to silence and were frightened. Even Rachel did not say a word: she had no reply to make. Then the little marquis put his champagne glass, which had just been refilled, on the head of the Jewess and exclaimed: 'All the women in France belong to us as well!'

At that she got up so quickly that the glass upset, spilling the amber-coloured wine on her black hair as if to baptize her, and broke into a hundred fragments as it fell to the floor. Her lips trembling, she defied the looks of the officer who was still laughing, and spluttered in a voice choked with rage: 'That – that – that – is not true – for you shall not have the women of France!'

He sat down again so as to laugh at his ease; and, trying to speak with the Parisian accent, he said: 'That is goot, wery goot! But why did you come here, my leetle one?'

She was speechless, and for a moment made no reply, for in her agitation she had not at first understood him. But as soon as she grasped his meaning she said to him indignantly and vehemently: 'I! I! I am not a woman, I am only a whore, and that's almost good enough for a Prussian.'

Almost before she had finished he slapped her full in the face; but as he was raising his hand again, as if to strike her, she seized from the table a small dessert knife with a silver blade and, mad with rage, stabbed him right in the hollow of his neck. Something that he was about to say died in his throat, and he sat there with his mouth half open and a terrible look in his eyes.

All the officers shouted in horror and jumped up wildly. Throwing her chair between the legs of Lieutenant Otto, who fell down at full length, she dashed to the window, opened it before they could seize her, and leaped out into the night and the pouring rain.

In two minutes Mademoiselle Fifi was dead. Fritz and Otto drew their swords and wanted to kill the women, who threw themselves at their feet and clung to their knees. With some difficulty the major prevented the slaughter and had the four terrified girls locked up in a room under the care of two soldiers. Then he organized the pursuit of the fugitive as carefully as if he were about to engage in a skirmish, feeling quite certain that she would be caught.

The table, which had been cleared immediately, now served as a bed on which to lay out the lieutenant.The four officers stood at the windows, stiffly and sobered, with the stern faces of soldiers on duty; and, through the steady torrent of rain, tried to penetrate the darkness of the night. Suddenly a shot was heard, and then another, a long way off; and for four hours they heard from time to time near or distant reports and rallying cries, and strange words of challenge, uttered in guttural voices.

In the morning they all returned. Two soldiers had been killed and three others wounded by their comrades in the ardour of that chase and in the confusion of that nocturnal pursuit; but they had not caught Rachel.

The inhabitants of the district were terrorized, the houses ransacked, and the country scoured over and over again, but the Jewess seemed not to have left a single trace of her flight behind her.

When the general was told of it he gave orders to hush up the affair, so as not to set a bad example to the army, but he severely censured the commandant, who in turn punished his inferiors. The general had said: 'One does not go to war in order to amuse oneself and paw prostitutes.' Count von Farlsberg, in his exasperation, made up his mind to have his revenge on the district, but as he required a pretext for showing severity, he sent for the priest and ordered him to have the bell tolled at the funeral of the Marquis von Eyrick.

Contrary to all expectation, the priest showed himself compliant and most respectful, and when Mademoiselle Fifi's body left the Château d'Uville on its way to the cemetery, carried by soldiers – preceded, surrounded and followed by soldiers who marched with loaded rifles – for the first time the bell sounded its funeral knell in a lively manner, as if a friendly hand were caressing it. At night it rang again, and the next day, and every day; it rang as much as anyone could desire. Sometimes even it would start at night and toll on gently through the darkness, seized with a strange joy, awakened one could not tell why. All the peasants in the neighbourhood declared that it was bewitched. Nobody except the priest and the sacristan would now go near the church tower. And they went because a poor girl was living there in terror and solitude and provided for secretly by those two men.

She remained there until the German troops departed, and then one evening the priest borrowed the baker's cart and himself drove his prisoner to Rouen. When they got there he embraced her, and she quickly went back on foot to her old establishment, where the proprietress, who thought that she was dead, was very glad to see her again.

A short time afterwards a patriot who had no prejudices, who liked her because of her bold deed, and who afterwards loved her for herself, married her and made of her a lady quite as good as many others so described.

THE NECKLACE

$\mathbf{S}$he was one of those pretty and charming young girls who continue to be born from time to time, as if by a slip of fate, into a family of clerks. She had no dowry, no expectations, no means of coming across any rich and distinguished man who would understand, love and marry her. She let herself be married to a minor civil servant in the Ministry of Education.

She dressed simply since she could hardly afford better, but she was every bit as unhappy as if she had really come down in the world. With women there is neither caste nor rank, for beauty, grace and charm take the place of birth and breeding. Natural ingenuity, instinct for the elegant, a supple mind are their sole hierarchy, and often make of women of the common people the equals of the very greatest ladies.

Mathilde suffered ceaselessly, feeling herself intended for the delicacies and luxuries of life. She was distressed at the poverty of her pension, at the bareness of the walls, at the shabby chairs, the ugly curtains. All these things, of which another woman of her rank would never even have been conscious, tortured her and made her angry. The sight of the little Breton peasant-girl who did her household chores stirred in her despairing regrets and impossible fantasies. She mused on silent antechambers hung with Oriental tapestries, lit by tall bronze candelabra, and of two fine footmen in knee breeches asleep in the deep armchairs, drowsy with the pervasive warmth of the stove. She dreamed of great salons hung with ancient silk, of the dainty cabinets containing priceless curiosities and of little gemütlich perfumed reception rooms made for chatting at five in the afternoon with intimate friends, with men celebrated and sought after, whom all women envy and whose attention they all desire.

When she sat down to supper at the round table covered with a tablecloth in use three days, opposite her husband, who uncovered the soup tureen and declared with a delighted air, 'Ah, stew! I don't know anything better', she thought of dainty dinners, of glittering silverware, of tapestry that peopled the walls with mythical personages and with strange birds flitting in a fairy forest; and she thought of delicious dishes served on exquisite porcelain and of the whispered gallantries to which you listen with a sphinx-like smile while you are eating the wings of a quail or the pink flesh of a trout.

She had no evening dresses, no jewels, nothing. And that was all she loved. It was what she was made for. She would have liked so much to please, to be envied, to be charming, to be sought after.

She had a friend, a former schoolmate at the convent, who was rich, and whom she did not like to go to see any more because she felt so depressed when she got home.

Then one evening her husband came home with a triumphant air, holding a large envelope in his hand. 'There', said he, 'there's something for you.'

She opened the envelope immediatly and drew out a printed card which bore these words:

The Minister of Public Instruction and Madame Georges Ramponneau request the honour of M. and Madame Loisel's company at the palace of the Ministry on Monday evening, January 18th.

Instead of being delighted, as her husband had hoped, she threw the invitation on the table crossly, muttering: 'What do you suppose I can do with that?'

'Why, my dear, I thought you'd be glad. You never go out, and this is such a splendid opportunity. I had to go to great lengths getting it. Everyone wants to go; it is very select, and they aren't giving many invitations to underlings. The whole official world will be there. You'll be able to see all the big cheeses there.'

She looked at him with an irritated glance and said brusquely: 'And what do you wish me to put on my back?'

He had not thought of that. He burst out: 'Why, the dress you go to the theatre in. It looks perfectly okay to me.'

He stopped, stupefied, lost at the sight of his wife weeping. Two great tears ran slowly from the corners of her eyes towards the corners of her mouth.

'What's up? What's got into you?' he asked.

By a violent effort she quelled her distress and replied in a calm voice, as she wiped away her tears: 'Nothing. Only I have nothing to wear, and, so, I can't go to this party. Give your card to some colleague whose wife is better equipped than I am.'

He was devastated. 'Come, let us see, Mathilde,' he pressed her, 'how much would it cost, a suitable dress, which you could use on other occasions – something quite simple?'

She reflected several seconds, making her calculations and wondering also what sum she could ask without drawing on herself an immediate refusal and a shocked exclamation from the frugal clerk.

Finally she replied hesitatingly: 'I don't know exactly, but I think I could manage it with four hundred francs.'

He grew a little pale, since he was laying aside just that amount to buy a gun and treat himself to a little shooting next summer on the plain of Nanterre with several friends who went there on Sundays to shoot larks

But he said: 'Very well. I will give you four hundred francs. And try to come up with a pretty dress.'

The day of the party drew near and Madame Loisel seemed really down, unsettled, anxious. Her frock however was ready. Her husband said to her one evening: 'What's the matter? Come, you've been acting so strange these last three days.'

She answered: 'It bothers me not having a single piece of jewellery, not a single gem, nothing to put on. I shall look like a church mouse. I would almost rather not go at all.'

'You could wear fresh flowers,' said her husband. 'They're quite fashionable at this time of year. For ten francs you can get two or three magnificent roses.'

She was not convinced.

'No; there's nothing more humiliating than to look poor among other women who are well off.'

'How daft you are!' her husband exclaimed. 'Go and see your friend Madame Forestier and ask her to lend you some jewellery. You know her well enough to do that.'

She uttered a delighted exclamation. 'I never thought of that!'

The next day she went to her friend and told her of her distress.

Madame Forestier went to a her mirrored wardrobe, took out a large jewel box, brought it back, opened it up and said to Madame Loisel: 'Choose, my dear.'

She saw first some bracelets, then a pearl necklace, then a Venetian gold cross set with precious stones, of admirable workmanship. She tried on the necklaces in front of the mirror, hesitated and could hardly bear to part with them, to hand them back. She kept asking: 'Haven't you anything else?'

'Why, yes. Keep looking; I don't know what you fancy.'

Suddenly she came across, in a black satin box, a superb diamond necklace, and her heart throbbed with a rampant desire. Her hands trembled as she took it. She fastened it round her throat and was lost in ecstasy at her reflection in the mirror.

Tremulously she asked: 'Will you lend me this, just this?'

'Why, yes, certainly.'

She threw her arms round her friend's neck, kissed her passionately, then fled with her treasure.

The night of the ball arrived. Madame Loisel was a success. She was the prettiest of the lot, elegant, graceful, glowing and touched with joy. All the fellows looked at her, asked her name, sought to be introduced. All secretaries of the Cabinet wished to waltz with her. She was noticed by the minister himself.

She danced with rapture, with abandon, intoxicated with pleasure, oblivious of all else in the triumph of her beauty, in the glory of her success, in a sort of cloud of happiness composed of all this homage and admiration, and of that sense of conquest which is so sweet to woman's heart.

She left the ball about four o'clock in the morning. Her husband had been snoozing since midnight in a little neglected parlour with three other gentlemen whose wives were having a good time at the ball.

He threw over her shoulders the wraps he had brought, the modest wraps of common life, the dowdiness of which contrasted with the elegance of the evening dress. She felt this sharply and wished to slip away without being noticed by the other women, enveloping themselves in costly furs.

Loisel held her back, saying: 'Hang on a bit. You'll catch cold outside. I'll call a cab.'

She would not listen to him and hastily descended the stairs. Outside in the street they could find no car. Searching for one, they tried hailing cabbies passing in the distance.

They walked towards the Seine in some desperation, shivering with cold. At last they found on the embankment one of those ancient nocturnal cabs which, rather as though they were ashamed to show their shabbiness during the day, are never seen round Paris until after nightfall.

It took them to their place in the Rue des Martyrs, and heavily they mounted the stairs to their flat. It was all over for her. As for him, he was aware that he must be at the ministry at ten o'clock that morning.

She took off her wraps in front of the glass for one more glimpse of herself in all her glory. But suddenly she uttered a cry. The necklace was no longer round her neck!

'What is the matter with you?' demanded her husband, already half undressed.

She turned distractedly towards him.

'I've – I've – I've lost Madame Forestier's necklace', she cried.

He straightened up, shattered.

'How on earth … ? Impossible!'

They looked among the folds of her skirt, of her wraps, in her pockets, everywhere. They did not find it.

'You're sure you had it on when you left the ball?' he asked.

'Yes, I remember feeling it in the hallway of the minister's house.'

'But if you'd lost it in the street we'd have heard it fall. It must be in the cab.'

'Yes, probably. Did you get the number?'

'No. And you – did you?'

'No.'

They looked, speechless, at each other. At last Loisel put on his clothes.

'I shall go back on foot', said he, 'the whole way we came, to see whether I can find it.'

He went out. She sat waiting on a chair in her evening dress, without strength to go to bed, stunned, without any fire in the grate, mindless.

Her husband got back about seven o'clock. He had found nothing.

He went to police headquarters, to the newspaper offices to offer a reward; he went to the cab companies – everywhere, in fact, the least spark of hope took him.

She waited all day, in the same condition of insane fear in the face of this ghastly calamity.

Loisel returned that evening with a hollow, ashen face. He had discovered nothing.

'You must write to your friend', said he, 'and say you've broken the clasp of her necklace and you're having it mended. That will give us time to work things out.'

She wrote at his dictation.

By the end of a week they had lost all hope. Loisel, who had aged five years, declared: 'We must start thinking how to replace that necklace.'

Next day they took the box that had contained it and went to the jeweller whose name was inside. He consulted his order book.

'It was not I, madame, who sold that necklace; I must simply have provided the case.'

Then they went from jeweller to jeweller, searching for a necklace like it, trying, struggling to recall it, both of them sick with chagrin and grief.

In a shop at the Palais Royal, they did find a diamond collar that seemed to them exactly like the one they were looking for. It was worth forty thousand francs. They could have it for thirty-six.

They begged the jeweller not to sell it for three days. And they made a deal that he should buy it back for thirty-four thousand francs, in case they should find the lost necklace before the end of February.

Loisel had eighteen thousand francs which his father had left him. The rest he would have to borrow.

He did borrow, a thousand francs here, five hundred there, five louis here, three louis there. He gave promissory notes, accepted ruinous terms, dealt with sharks and all the race of money-lenders. He mortgaged the rest of his life, signing papers without a notion as to whether he could meet the obligation; and sick with worry at trouble yet to come, at the black misery about to engulf him, at the prospect of all the physical privations and moral tortures he was to suffer, he went to fetch the new necklace, laying upon the jeweller's counter thirty-six thousand francs.

When Madame Loisel took back the necklace, Madame Forestier said to her with coldly: 'You should have returned it sooner; I might have needed it.'

She did not open the case, as her friend had so much feared. If she had detected the substitution, what might she have said, what would she have said? Would she not have taken Madame Loisel for a thief?

Thereafter Madame Loisel knew the grim existence of the needy. She bore her part, however, with sudden heroism. That dreadful debt must be paid. She would pay it. They dismissed their servant; they changed their lodgings; they rented a garret under the roof.

She came to know what heavy housework meant and the odious demands of the kitchen. She washed dishes, putting to use her dainty fingers and rosy nails on greasy pots and pans. She washed soiled linen and the shirts and the dishcloths, which she dried on a line; she took the slops down to the street every morning and brought up the water, stopping for breath at every landing. And dressed like a woman of the people, she went to the fruiterer, the grocer, the butcher, a basket on her arm, haggling, insulted to her face, defending her pittance, sou by sou.

Every month they had to meet some notes, renew others, extract more time.

Her husband worked in the evenings, making up some tradesman's accounts, and late at night he often copied manuscript for five sous a page.

This life lasted ten years.

At the end of ten years they had paid everything, everything at usurious rates and relentless accumulations of compound interest.

Madame Loisel looked old now. She had become the woman of impoverished households – strong and hard and rough. With frowsy hair, skirts askew and red hands, she talked loud while washing the floor with great swooshes of water. But sometimes, when her husband was at the office, she sat down near the window and thought of that fun evening of long ago, of that ball where she had looked so beautiful and been so much admired.

What would have happened if she had not lost that necklace? Who knows? who knows? How strange and changeful is life! How small a thing is needed to make or ruin us!

Then one Sunday, having set off for a walk in the Champs Elysées to restore herself after the labours of the week, she suddenly saw a woman leading a child by the hand. It was Madame Forestier, still young, still beautiful, still charming.

Madame Loisel felt moved. Should she speak to her? Yes, certainly. And now that she had paid, she would tell her all about it. Why not?

She went up.

'Good day, Jeanne.'

The other, astonished to be familiarly addressed by so common a woman, failed to recognize her at all and stammered: 'But – madame! – I 'm sorry – I don't think I know … you must be mistaken.'

'No. I am Mathilde Loisel.'

Her friend uttered a cry. 'Oh, my poor Mathilde! How you've changed!'

'Yes, I have had a very hard life, since I last saw you, and great poverty – and that's because of you!'

'Of me! How come?'

'D'you remember that diamond necklace you lent me to wear at the ministerial ball?'

'Yes. What of it?'

'Well, I lost it.'

'What do you mean? You brought it back.'

'I brought you back another exactly like it. And it has taken us ten years to pay for it. You can understand that it was not easy for us, for us who had nothing. At last it is ended, and I am very glad.'

Madame Forestier had stopped.

'You say that you bought a necklace of diamonds to replace mine?'

'Yes. You never noticed it, then! They were very similar.' And she smiled with a joy that was at once proud and ingenuous.

Madame Forestier, deeply moved, took both her hands.

'Oh, my poor Mathilde! Why, my necklace was paste! It couldn't have been worth more than five hundred francs!'

THE PIECE OF STRING

It was market-day, and from all the country around Goderville the peasants and their wives were coming towards the town. The men walked slowly, their bodies tilted forward with every step of their long, bandy legs. They were deformed from handling the plough which makes the left shoulder higher and twists the spine; from mowing the corn, when they have to spread their legs so as to keep on their feet. Their starched blue smocks, glossy as if varnished, ornamented at collar and cuffs with a little embroidered design and blown out round their bony bodies, looked very much like balloons, whence issued two arms and two feet.

Some of these fellows led a cow or a calf at the end of a rope. And just behind the animal followed their wives switching it accross the back with a leaf-covered branch to sharpen up its pace, and carrying large baskets out of which protruded the heads of chickens or ducks. These women walked more quickly and energetically than the men, their erect, gaunt figures adorned with scanty little shawls pinned over flat bosoms, and their heads wrapped round with a white cloth, enclosing the hair and surmounted by a bonnet.

Now a wagonette passed by, jogging along behind a horse and shaking up the two men on the seat, and the woman at the bottom of the cart who held fast to its sides to lessen the hard jolting.

In the market-place at Goderville was a great crowd, a mingled multitude of men and beasts. The horns of cattle, the high, beaver hats of wealthy peasants, the head-dresses of the women, stood out above the throng. And the sharp, shrill, yakety-yak of voices made a continuous, wild din, while above it occasionally rose a huge burst of laughter from the sturdy lungs of a merry peasant or a prolonged bellow from a cow tied fast to the wall of a house.

It all smelt of the stable, of milk, hay and perspiration, giving off that half-human, half-animal odour peculiar to folks who work the land.

Maître Hauchecorne, of Bréauté, had just arrived at Goderville and was making his way towards the square when he noticed on the ground a little piece of string. Maître Hauchecorne, economical as are all true Normans, reflected that everything was worth picking up which could be of any use, and he stooped down, painfully, because he suffered from rheumatism. He took up the bit of thin string from the ground and was carefully preparing to roll it up when he saw Maître Malandain, the harness-maker, on his doorstep gazing at him. They had once had a quarrel about a halter, and they had borne each other malice ever since. Maître Hauchecorne was overcome with a sort of shame at being seen by his enemy picking up a piece of string on the road. He quickly hid it beneath his blouse and then slipped it into his breeches pocket, pretending to be still looking for something on the ground which he did not discover, and finally went off towards the market-place, his head bent forward and his body almost doubled in two by the rheumatism.

He was at once lost in the crowd, which kept circulating slowly and noisily as it bartered and bargained. The peasants examined the cows, went off, came back, always in doubt for fear of being cheated, never quite daring to decide, looking the seller square in the eye in the effort to discover the tricks of the man and the defect in the animal.

The women, having placed their great baskets at their feet, had taken out the poultry, which lay upon the ground, legs tied together, their eyes terrified and combs scarlet.

They listened to propositions, maintaining their prices in a decided manner with an impassive face or perhaps deciding to accept the smaller price offered, suddenly calling out to the customer who was starting to go away: 'All right, I'll let you have them, Maît' Anthime.'

Then, little by little, the square became empty, and when the Angelus struck midday those who lived at a distance poured into the inns.

At Jourdain's the great room was filled with diners, just as the vast court was filled with vehicles of every sort – wagons, gigs, carts, tilburies, innumerable vehicles which have no name, yellow with mud, misshapen, pieced together, some raising their shafts to heaven like two arms, some with their noses on the ground and tails in the air.

Just accross from where the diners were at table the huge fireplace with its bright flames gave out a burning heat to warm the backs of those who sat at the right. Three spits were turning, primed with chickens, pigeons and joints of mutton, and a delectable odour of roast meat, and of gravy flowing over crisp brown skin, arising from the hearth, kindled merriment and had mouths watering.

All the aristocracy of the plough were eating there at Maît' Jourdain's, innkeeper and horse-dealer, a sharp fellow who had made a great deal of money in his day.

Dishes were passed round and emptied, as were the jugs of yellow cider. Everyone told of his affairs, of what he had bought and sold. They exchanged news about the crops. The weather was good for green stuff, but too wet for grain.

Suddenly the drumroll began in the courtyard in front of the house; and they all, except some of the most blasé, were on their feet at once and ran to the door, to the windows, their mouths full and napkins in their hand.

When the public crier had finished his tattoo he called forth in a jerky voice, pausing in the wrong places: 'Be it known to the inhabitants of Goderville and in general to all persons present at the market that there has been lost this morning on the Beuzeville road, between nine and ten o'clock, a black leather pocket-book containing five hundred francs and business papers. You are requested to return it to the mayor's office at once or to Maître Fortuné Houlbrèque, of Manneville. There will be twenty francs reward.'

Then the man went away. They heard once more at a distance the roll of the drum and the faint voice of the crier. Then they all began to talk of this incident, reckoning up the chances Maître Houlbrèque had of recovering his pocket-book or not.

The meal went on. They were finishing their coffee when the corporal of gendarmes appeared on the threshold.

He asked: 'Is Maître Hauchecorne of Bréauté here?'

Maître Hauchecorne, seated at the other end of the table, answered: 'Here I am, here I am.'

'Would you be kind enough to come with me to the Town Hall? The Mayor would like a word.'

He followed the corporal.

The mayor was waiting for him, seated in an armchair. He was the notary of the place, a tall, grave man of pompous speech.

'Maître Hauchecorne,' said he, 'this morning on the Beuzeville road, you were seen to pick up the pocket-book lost by Maître Houlbrèque, of Manneville.'

The countryman looked at the mayor in amazement, frightened already at this suspicion which rested on him, he knew not why.

'I – I picked up that pocket-book?'

'Yes, you.'

'I swear I know nothing about it.'

'You were seen.'

'I was seen – I? Who saw me?'

'Monsieur Malandain, the harness-maker.'

Then the old man remembered, understood, and, reddening with anger, said: 'Ah! he saw me, did he, the rascal? He saw me picking up this string here, M'sieu le Maire.'

And fumbling at the bottom of his pocket, he pulled out of it the little end of string.

But the mayor incredulously shook his head: 'You will not make me believe, Maître Hauchecorne, that Monsieur Malandain, who is a man whose word can be relied on, has mistaken this string for a pocketbook.'

The peasant, furious, raised his hand and spat on the ground beside him as if to attest his good faith, repeating: 'For all that, it is God's truth, M'sieu le Maire. There! On my soul's salvation, I repeat it.'

The mayor continued: 'After you picked up the object in question, you even looked about for some time in the mud to see if a piece of money had not dropped out of it.'

The good man was choking with indignation and alarm.

'How can anyone tell – how can they tell such lies, to slander an honest man! How can they?'

His protestations were in vain; he was not believed.

He was confronted with Monsieur Malandain, who repeated and persisted with his testimony. They railed at one another for an hour. At his own request Maître Hauchecorne was searched. Nothing was found on him.

At last the mayor, much perplexed, sent him away, warning him that he would inform the public prosecutor and ask for instructions.

The news had spread. When he left the mayor's office the old man was surrounded by people, interrogating him with a curiosity which was serious or mocking, as the case might be, but in which no indignation was present. He began to tell the story of the string. They did not believe him. They laughed.

He moved along, buttonholed by everyone, himself buttonholing his acquaintances, beginning over and over again his tale and his protestations, showing his pockets turned inside out to prove he had nothing in them. They said to him: 'You old rogue!'

He grew more and more angry, disturbed, in despair at not being believed, and kept on telling his story.

Night came: it was time to go home. He left with three of his neighbours, to whom he pointed out the place where he had picked up the string, and all the way he talked of nothing else.

That evening he made the round of the village of Bréauté for the purpose of telling everyone. He met only unbelievers.

All night long he brooded over it.

The next day, about one in the afternoon, Marius Paumelle, a farm hand of Maître Breton, the market gardener at Ymauville, returned the pocket-book and its contents to Maître Holbreque of Manneville.

This man said, indeed, that he had found it on the road, but not knowing how to read, he had carried it home and given it to his employer.

The news spread around the neighborhood. Maître Hauchecorne was informed. He started off at once and began to relate his story with the dénouement. He was triumphant.

'What grieved me,' said he, 'was not the thing itself, do you understand, but it was being accused of lying. Nothing does you so much harm as being in disgrace for lying.'

All day he talked of his adventure. He told it to those who passed by on the road, people drinking at the inn, and next Sunday to more coming out of the church. He even stopped strangers to tell them about it. He was easy now, and yet something worried him without his knowing exactly what it was. People had a jokey manner while they listened. They did not seem convinced. He seemed to feel their remarks behind his back.

On Tuesday of the following week he went to market at Goderville, prompted solely by the need of telling his story.

Malandain, standing on his doorstep, began to laugh as he saw him pass. Why?

He accosted a farmer of Criquetot, who did not let him finish, and giving him a mock punch in the pit of the stomach, exclaimed in his face: 'Oh, you great rogue!' Then the farmer turned on his heels.

Maître Hauchecorne grew more and more uneasy. Why would they have called him a 'great rogue'?

When seated at table in Jourdain's tavern he began again to explain the whole affair.

A horse dealer of Montivilliers shouted at him: 'Get out, get out, you old scamp! I know all about your piece of string.'

Hauchecorne stammered: 'But they found it, the pocket-book!'

But the other continued: 'Hold your tongue; there's one who finds it and there's another who returns it. And no one's the wiser.'

The farmer was speechless. He understood at last. They accused him of having had the pocket-book brought back by an accomplice, by a confederate.

He tried to protest. The whole table began to laugh.

He could not finish his dinner, and went away amid a chorus of jeers.

He went home indignant, choking with rage, with confusion, the more cast down since with his Norman craftiness he was, perhaps, capable of having done what they accused him of and even of boasting of it as a good trick. He was dimly conscious that it was impossible to prove his innocence, his duplicity being so well known. He felt himself struck to the heart by the injustice of the suspicion.

He began anew to tell his tale, lengthening his recital every day, each day adding new proofs, more energetic declarations and more sacred oaths, which he thought out and prepared in his hours of solitude, for his mind was entirely occupied with the story of the string. The more he denied it, the more artful his arguments, the less he was believed.

'Those are liars' proofs,' they said behind his back.

He felt this. It preyed upon him and he exhausted himself in useless effort.

He was visibly wasting away.

Jokers would make him tell the story of 'the piece of string' for their own amusement, just as you get a soldier who has been on a campaign tell his story of the battle. His mind was growing weaker, and about the end of December he took to his bed.

He passed away early in January, and, in the ravings of death agony, he was protesting his innocence, repeating: 'A little piece of string – a little piece of string. See, here it is, M'sieu le Maire…'

THAT PIG OF A MORIN

i

'There my friend', I said to Labarbe, 'you have just repeated those five words, *that pig of a Morin*. Why on earth do I never hear Morin's name mentioned without his being called a pig?'

Labarbe, a deputy, looked at me with his owl-like gaze and said; 'Do you mean to say that you don't know Morin's story and you come from La Rochelle?'

I was obliged to infer that I did not know Morin's story, so Labarbe began his recital.

'You knew Morin, did you not, and you remember his large linen-draper's shop on the Quai de La Rochelle?'

'Yes, perfectly.'

'Well, then. You must know that some years ago Morin went to spend a fortnight in Paris for pleasure, or for his pleasures, but under the pretext of replenishing his stock, and you also know what a fortnight in Paris means to a country shopkeeper. It inflames his blood. The theatre every evening, women's dresses rustling up against you and continual arousal; one goes almost mad with it. One sees nothing but dancers in tights, actresses in very low dresses, shapely legs, bare shoulders, all nearly within reach of one's hands, without one daring or being able to touch them. When one leaves the city one's heart is still all in a flutter and one's mind still exhilarated by a yearning for kisses.

'Morin was in that condition when he took his ticket for La Rochelle by the 8.40 night express. As he was walking up and down the waiting-room at the station he stopped suddenly in front of a young lady giving a kiss to an older one. She had her veil up, and Morin murmured with delight: "By Jove, there's a pretty woman!"

'When she had said her goodbyes to the old lady and gone into the waiting-room Morin followed her; then she went out on the platform and Morin still followed her. She got into an empty carriage, and Morin once more followed her. There were very few travellers on the express. The engine whistled and the train started. They were alone. Morin devoured her with his eyes. She appeared to be about nineteen or twenty and was fair, tall, with a bold look. She wrapped a rug round her and stretched herself on the seat to sleep.

'Morin asked himself: *I wonder who she is?* And a thousand conjectures, a thousand notions ran through his head. He said to himself: "So many adventures are told as happening on railway journeys that this may be one that is going to come my way. Who knows? A piece of good luck like that happens very suddenly, and perhaps I need only be a little venturesome. Was it not Danton who said: 'Audacity, more audacity and always audacity'? If it wasn't Danton it was Mirabeau, not that it matters. But then I have no audacity, and that's the difficulty. Oh! If one only knew, if one could only read people's minds! I will bet that every day one passes up magnificent opportunities without knowing it, though a gesture would be enough to let me know her mind."

'He began to imagine himself in situations which led him to triumph. He pictured some chivalrous deed or merely some slight service which he rendered her, a lively, gallant conversation which ended in a declaration.

'But he could find no opening, had no pretext, and he waited for some fortunate development, with his heart beating and his mind racing. The night passed and the pretty girl slept on, while Morin contemplated his own failure. Day broke and soon the first ray of sunlight appeared, a long, clear ray which shone on the face of the sleeping girl and woke her. She sat up, looked at the country, then at Morin and smiled. She smiled like a happy woman, with a bright engaging look, and Morin trembled. Certainly that smile was intended for him; it was discreet invitation, the signal which he was waiting for. That smile meant to say: "How stupid, what a dolt you are, to have sat there on your seat like a post all night! Just look at me, am I not charming? And you have sat like that for the whole night, when you have been alone with a pretty woman, you great simpleton!"

'She was still smiling as she looked at him; and even began to chuckle. He lost his head trying to find something suitable to say, no matter what. But he could think of nothing, nothing, until, seized with a coward's courage, he said to himself: "So much the worse, I will risk everything." All at once, without the slightest warning, he went towards her, arms extended, lips protruding, and, seizing her in his arms, tried to kiss her.

'She sprang up immediately with a bound, yelling: "Help! help!" and screaming with terror. Then she opened the carriage door and waved her arm, mad with terror and trying to jump out while Morin, virtually beside himself, held her by the skirt and stammered; "Oh, madame! Oh, madame!"

'The train slackened speed and came to a halt. Two guards rushed up at the young woman's frantic signals. She threw herself into their arms, stammering: "That man wanted – wanted to – to –" And then she fainted.

'They were at Mauzé station, and the gendarme on duty arrested Morin. When the victim of his indiscreet admiration had regained her consciousness, she made her charge against him, and the police drew it up. The poor linen-draper did not reach home till night; and there was a prosecution hanging over him for an outrage to morals in a public place.

ii

'At that time I was editor of the *Fanal des Charentes*, and I would meet Morin every day at the Café du Commerce. The day after his misadventure he came to see me. He did not know what to do. I didn't hide my opinion from him, and put it to him: "You are no better than a pig. No decent man behaves like that."

'He cried. His wife had given him a beating, and he foresaw his trade ruined, his name dragged through the mire and dishonoured, his friends scandalized and ostracizing him. In the end he excited my pity, and I sent for my colleague, Rivet, a jocular but very sensible little man, to give us his advice.

'He advised me to see the public prosecutor, who was a friend of mine, and so I sent Morin home and went to call on the magistrate. He told me that the young lady who had been insulted was a Mademoiselle Henriette Bonnel, who had just received her certificate as governess in Paris and was spending her holidays with her uncle and aunt, very respectable tradespeople in Mauzé. What made Morin's case all the more serious was that the uncle had lodged the complaint. However, the public prosecutor had consented to let the matter drop if this complaint were withdrawn; so we must try and get him to do just that.

'I went back to Morin's and found him in bed, ill with nervous exhaustion and distress. His wife, a tall raw-boned woman with a beard, was abusing him continually, and she showed me into the room, shouting at me: "So you have come to see that pig of a Morin. Well, there he is!" And she planted herself at the foot of the bed, with her hands on her hips. I told him how matters stood, and he begged me to go and see the girl's uncle and aunt. It was a delicate mission, but I undertook it, and the poor devil never ceased repeating: "I assure you I did not even kiss her; no, not so much as that. I swear to it!"

'I replied: "It is all the same; you are nothing but a pig." And I took a thousand francs which he gave me to make use of as I thought best. But as I did not care to venture to her uncle's house alone, I begged Rivet to come with me, which he agreed to do on condition that we went immediately, since he had urgent business at La Rochelle that afternoon. So two hours later we rang at the door of a pretty country house. An attractive girl came and opened the door to us, assuredly the young lady in question, and I said to Rivet in a low voice: "Confound it! I begin to understand Morin!"

The uncle, Monsieur Tonnelet, subscribed to the *Fanal*, and was a fervent political co-religionist of ours. He received us with open arms and congratulated us and wished us joy, delighted at having the two editors in his house. Rivet whispered to me: "I think we shall be able to arrange the matter of that pig of a Morin for him."

'The niece had left the room and I introduced the delicate subject. I waved the spectre of scandal before his eyes; I emphasised the inevitable besmirching which the young lady would suffer if such an affair became known, for nobody would believe in a mere kiss. The good man seemed undecided, but he could not make up his mind about anything without his wife, who would not be in until late that evening. Then suddenly he uttered an exclamation of triumph: "Look here, I have an excellent idea; I'll keep you here to dine and stay the night, and when my wife comes home I hope we shall be able to arrange matters."

'Rivet resisted at first, but the desire to extricate Morin decided him. We accepted the invitation. The uncle stood up delighted, called his niece and proposed that we should take a stroll in his grounds, saying: "We'll leave serious matters til the morning." Rivet and he began to talk politics, while I soon found myself lagging a little behind with the girl who was really charming, and with the greatest precaution I began to speak to her about her adventure and try to make her my ally. She did not, however, appear in the least confused, and listened to me like a person who was enjoying the whole thing very much.

'I was saying to her: "Just think, mademoiselle, how unpleasant it will be for you. You will have to appear in court, to encounter malicious looks, to speak in front of everybody and to recount that unfortunate occurrence in the railway carriage in public. Don't you think, between ourselves, that it would have been much better for you to have put that dirty scoundrel back in his place without calling for assistance?" She began to laugh and replied: "What you say is quite true, but what could I do? I was frightened, and when one is frightened one does not stop to reason with oneself. As soon as I realized the situation I was really sorry that I had called out, but then it was too late. You must also remember that the idiot threw himself upon me like a madman, without saying a word and looking like a lunatic. I didn't even know what he wanted of me."

'She looked me full in the face without being nervous, and I said to myself: "She's a queer sort of girl. I can quite see how Morin came to make a mistake." I went on jokingly: "Come, mademoiselle, confess that it was excusable, for, after all, a man cannot find himself opposite such a pretty girl as you are without feeling a natural desire to kiss her."

'She laughed more than ever and showed her teeth and said: "Between the desire and the act, monsieur, there is room for respect." It was an odd way to put it, and not very clear. I asked abruptly: "Well, now, suppose I were to kiss you, what would you do?" She stopped to look at me from head to foot and then said calmly: "Oh, you? That is quite another matter."

'I knew perfectly well that it was not the same thing at all, as everybody in the neighbourhood called me "Handsome Labarbe" – I was thirty years old in those days – but I asked her: "And why, pray?" She shrugged her shoulders and replied: "Well! because you are not so stupid as he is." And then she added, looking at me slyly, "Nor so ugly, either." And before she could make a movement to avoid me I had implanted a hearty kiss on her cheek. She sprang aside, but it was too late, and then she said: "Well, you aren't very bashful, either! But don't do that sort of thing again."

'I put on a humble look and said in a low voice: "Oh, mademoiselle! as for me, if I long for one thing more than another it is to be summoned before a magistrate for the same reason as Morin."

"Why?" she asked. And, looking steadily at her, I replied: "Because you are one of the most beautiful creatures living; because it would be an honour and a glory for me to have wished to offer you violence, and because people would have said, after seeing you: 'Well, Labarbe has richly deserved what he has got, but he is a lucky fellow, all the same.'"

'She began to laugh heartily again and said: "How funny you are!" And she had not finished the word "funny" before I had her in my arms and was kissing her ardently wherever I could find a place, on her forehead, on her eyes, on her lips occasionally, on her cheeks, all over her head, part of which she was obliged to leave exposed, in spite of herself, to defend the others. At last she managed to release herself, blushing and angry. "You are very unmannerly, monsieur," she said, "and I am sorry I gave attention to you."

'I took her hand in some confusion and stammered out: "I beg your pardon. I beg your pardon, mademoiselle. I have offended you; I have acted like a brute! Do not be angry with me for what I have done. If you knew – " I vainly sought for some excuse, and a moment later she said: "There is nothing for me to know, monsieur." But I had found something to say, and I exclaimed: "Mademoiselle, I love you!"

'She was really surprised and raised her eyes to look at me, and I went on, "Yes, mademoiselle, and please listen to me. I don't know Morin, and I don't care about him one way or the other. It does not matter to me in the least if he is committed for trial and locked up meanwhile. I saw you here last year, and I was so taken with you that the thought of you has never left me since, and it does not matter to me whether you believe me or not. I thought you adorable, and the memory of you took such a hold on me that I longed to see you again. I made use of that fool Morin as a pretext, and here I am. Circumstances have made me exceed the due limits of respect, and I can only ask you to forgive me."

'She looked at me to see if I was in earnest and was ready to smile again. Then she murmured: "You humbug!" But I raised my hand and said in a sincere voice (and I really believe I was sincere): "I swear to you that I am speaking the truth," and she simply replied : "Don't talk nonsense!"

'We were alone, quite alone, as Rivet and her uncle had disappeared down a path, and I made her a real declaration of love, while I squeezed and kissed her hands, and she listened to it as to something new and agreeable, without exactly knowing how much of it to believe, while in the end I felt agitated, and at last really myself believed what I said. I was pale, anxious and trembling, and I gently put my arm round her waist and spoke to her softly, whispering into the little curls over her ears. She seemed in a trance, so absorbed in thought was she.

'Then her hand touched mine, and she pressed it, and I gently squeezed her waist with a trembling, and gradually firmer, grasp. She didn't move now, and I touched her cheek with my lips, and suddenly without seeking them my lips met hers. It was a long, long kiss, and it would have lasted longer still if I had not heard a *hm! hm!* just behind me, at which she made her escape through the bushes, and turning round I saw Rivet coming towards me, and, standing in the middle of the path, he said without even smiling: "So that is the way you settle the affair of that pig of a Morin." And I replied conceitedly: "One does what one can, my dear fellow. But what about the uncle? How have you got on with him? I'll answer for the niece."

"I have not been so fortunate with him," he replied.

'Whereupon I took his arm and we went indoors.'

iii

'Dinner made me lose my head altogether. I sat beside her, and my hand continually met hers under the tablecloth; my foot touched hers and our glances met.

'After dinner we took a walk by moonlight, and I whispered all the tender things I could think of to her. I held her close to me, kissed her every moment, while her uncle and Rivet were arguing as they walked in front of us. They went in, and soon a messenger brought a telegram from her aunt, saying that she would not return until the next morning at seven o'clock by the first train.

'"Very well, Henriette," her uncle said, "go and show the gentlemen their rooms." She showed Rivet his first, and he whispered to me: "There was no danger of her taking us into yours first." Then she took me to my room, and as soon as she was alone with me I took her in my arms again and tried to arouse her emotion; but when she saw the danger she escaped out of the room, and I retired, very much put out and excited and feeling rather foolish, for I knew that I wouldn't sleep much. I was wondering how I could have committed such a mistake when there was a gentle knock at my door, and on my asking who was there a low voice replied: "I."

'I dressed myself quickly and opened the door, and she came in. "I forgot to ask you what you take in the morning," she said; "chocolate, tea or coffee?" I put my arms round her impetuously and said, devouring her with kisses: "I will take – I will take – "

'But she freed herself from my arms, blew out my candle and disappeared leaving me alone in the dark, furious, trying to find some matches, unable to do so. At last I got some and I went into the passage, feeling half mad, with my candlestick in my hand.

'What was I about to do? I did not stop to reason. I only wanted to find her, and I would. I went a few steps without reflecting, but then I suddenly thought: "Suppose I should walk into the uncle's room, what would I say?" And I stood still, with my head a void and my heart beating. But in a few moments I thought of an answer: "Of course, I shall say that I was looking for Rivet's room to speak to him about an important matter." Then I began to inspect all the doors, trying to find hers, and at last I took hold of a handle at a venture, turned it and went in. There was Henriette, sitting on her bed and looking at me in tears. So I gently turned the key, and going up to her on tiptoe, I said: "I forgot to ask you for something to read, mademoiselle."

'I was stealthily returning to my room when a rough hand seized me and a voice – it was Rivet's – whispered in my ear: "So you have not yet quite settled that affair of Morin's?"

'At seven o'clock the next morning Henriette herself brought me a cup of chocolate. I never have drunk anything like it, soft, velvety, perfumed, delicious. I could hardly take away my lips from the cup, and she had hardly left the room when Rivet came in. He seemed nervous and irritable, like a man who had not slept, and he said to me crossly: "If you go on like this you will end by ruining that affair of Morin's!"

'At eight o'clock the aunt arrived. Our discussion was very brief; they withdrew their complaint, and I left five hundred francs for the poor of the town. They wanted to keep us for the day, and they arranged an excursion to go and see some ruins. Henriette made signs to me to stay, behind their back, and I accepted, but Rivet was determined to be off, and though I took him aside and begged and pleaded with him to do this for me, he appeared pretty well exasperated and kept saying to me: "I have had quite enough of Morin's affair, do you hear?"

'Of course I was obliged to leave also, and it was one of the hardest moments of my life. I could have gone on arranging that business as long as I lived, and when we were in the railway carriage, after shaking hands with her in silence, I said to Rivet: "You are a brute!" And he replied: "My dear fellow, you were beginning to annoy me."

'On getting to the *Fanal* office, I saw a crowd waiting for us, and as soon as they saw us they all exclaimed: "Well, have you settled the affair of that pig of a Morin?" All La Rochelle was excited about it, and Rivet, who had got over his ill humour on the journey, had great difficulty in keeping himself from laughing as he said: "Yes, we have managed it, thanks to Labarbe." And we went to Morin's.

'He was sitting in an easy chair with mustard plasters on his legs and cold bandages on his head, nearly dead with misery. He was coughing with the short cough of a dying man, without anyone knowing how he had caught it, and his wife looked at him like a tigress ready to eat him. As soon as he saw us he trembled so violently that his hands and knees shook, so I said to him at once: "It is all settled, you dirty scamp, but don't do such a thing again."

'He got up, choking, took my hands and kissed them as if they had belonged to a prince, cried, nearly fainted, embraced Rivet and even kissed Madame Morin, who gave him such a push as to send him staggering back into his chair; but he never got over the blow; his mind had been too much upset. In all the country round, moreover, he was called nothing but "that pig of a Morin", and the epithet went through him like a sword thrust every time he heard it. When a street boy called after him "Pig!" he turned his head instinctively. His friends also overwhelmed him with horrible jokes and used to ask him, whenever they were eating ham, "Is it a bit of yourself?" He died two years later.

'As for myself, when I was a candidate, twelve years afterwards, for the Chamber of Deputies, I called on the new notary at Tousserre, Monsieur Belloncle, to solicit his vote, and a tall, beautiful and buxom lady received me. "You do not know me now?" she said. And I stammered out: "Why – no – madame." "Henriette Bonnel." "Ah!" And I felt myself turning pale, while she seemed perfectly at her ease and looked at me with a smile. "As soon as she had left me alone with her husband he took both my hands, and, squeezing them as if he meant to crush them, said, "I have been intending to go and see you for a long while, my dear sir, since my wife has often talked to me about you. I know, yes I know in what painful circumstances you made her acquaintance, and I know also how perfectly you behaved, how full of delicacy, tact and devotion you showed yourself in the affair – " he hesitated and then spoke in a lower tone, as if he were to say something coarse, "in the affair of that pig of a Morin."'

THE HORLA

May 8.   What a glorious day! I have spent the whole morning lying on the grass in front of my house, under the enormous plane-tree that provides a complete canopy, shelter and shade fot it. I love this country, and I love living here because it is here I have my roots, those deep, subtle roots that hold a man to the place where his forefathers were born and died, hold him to ways of thought and thought and of eating, to customs and to particular dishes, to local turns of phrase, to the intonations of country voices, to the scent of the soil, the villages, and the very air itself.

I love this house of mine where I grew up. From my windows I see the Seine flowing alongside my garden, beyond the high road, almost at my door, the great, broad Seine, that runs from Rouen to Havre, strewn with passing boats.

Away to the left, the great city of Rouen, with its blue roofs lying under the bristling host of Gothic belfries. They are beyond numbers, frail or sturdy, dominated by the iron spire of the cathedral, and filled with bells that ring out in the limpid air of fine mornings sending me the sweet and far-off murmur of their iron tongues, a brazen song borne to me on the breeze, now louder, now softer, as it swells or dies away.

How beautiful this morning has been!

Towards eleven o'clock boats in a long convoy followed each other past my gate, behind a squat tug as small as a fly that wheezed painfully as it vomited thick clouds of smoke.

After two English yachts, whose crimson ensign rose and fell against the sky, came a splendid Brazilian three-master, all white, gloriously clean and glittering. The sight of this ship filled me with such joy that I saluted her, I can't think why.

May 11.   I have had a slight fever for the last few days; I feel ill, or rather, I feel unhappy.

Whence come these mysterious influences that change our happiness to dejection and our self-confidence to gloom? It is as if the air, the unseen air, were full of unknowable powers whose mysterious nearness we endure. I wake full of joy, my throat swelling with a longing to sing. Why? I go down to the riverside; and suddenly, after a short stroll, I come back home wretched as if some misfortune were awaiting me there. Why? Has a chill shudder, passing over my skin, shaken my nerve and darkened my spirit? Have the shapes of the clouds, or the colour of the day, the ever-changing colour of the visible world, troubled my mind as they slipped past my eyes? Does anyone know? Everything that surrounds us, everything we see unseeing, everything we brush past unwitting, everything that we touch impalpably, everything that we encounter unnoticing, has on us – on the organs of our bodies, and through them on our thoughts, on our very hearts – swift, surprising and inexplicable effects.

How deep it is, this mystery of the Invisible! We cannot fathom it with our poor senses, with our eyes that perceive neither the too small, nor the too great, nor the too near, nor the too distant, neither the inhabitants of a star, nor the inhabitants of a drop of water … or with our ears that deceive us, for they transmit the vibrations of the air to us as sonorous tones. They are fairies who by a miracle transmute movement into sound, and by this metamorphosis give birth to music, and turn into song the mute quivering of Nature … with our smell, feebler than a dog's … with our taste, that can only just detect the age of a wine.

If only we had other organs to work other miracles on our behalf, what would we not discover around us!

May 16. I am certainly ill. I was so well last month. I have a fever, a wicked fever, or rather, a feverish weakness that oppresses my mind as much as my body. All day and every day I suffer this frightful sense of imminent danger, this apprehension of impending ill or approaching death, this presentiment which is doubtless the warning signal of a lurking disease germinating in my blood and my flesh.

May 18. I have consulted my doctor, for I was getting no sleep. He found that my pulse is rapid, my eyes dilated, my nerves on edge, but no alarming symptom of any kind. I am to take douches and drink bromide of potassium.

May 25. No change. My case is truly strange. As night falls, an incomprehensible uneasiness fills me, as if the night had some dreadful menace for me. I dine in haste, then I try to read; but I don't understand the words: I can hardly make out the letters. So I walk up and down in my drawing-room, oppressed by a vague fear that I cannot throw off, fear of sleeping and fear of my bed.

About ten o'clock I go up to my room. The instant I am inside the room I double-lock the door and shut the windows; I am afraid … of what? I never dreaded anything before… I open my cupboards, I look under my bed; I listen … listen … for what? It's a queer thing that a mere physical ailment, some disorder in the blood perhaps, the jangling of a nerve thread, a slight congestion, the least disturbance in the functioning of this living machine of ours, so imperfect and so fragile, can make a melancholic of the happiest of men and coward of the bravest. Then I lie down, and wait for sleep as if I were waiting to be executed. I wait for it, dreading its approach; my heart beats, my legs tremble; my whole body shivers in the warmth of the bed-clothes, until the moment I fall suddenly upon sleep, like a man falling into deep and stagnant waters, there to drown. I never feel it come as I used to, this perfidious sleep, that lurks close to me, spying on me, ready to take me by the head, shut my eyes, wipe me out.

I sleep – for a long time – two or three hours – then a dream – no: a nightmare seizes me. I feel that I am lying down and that I am asleep … I feel it and I know it … and I feel someone approaching me, looking at me, touching me, climbing on my bed, kneeling on my chest, taking my neck between his hands and squeezing … squeezing … with all his might, strangling me.

I struggle madly, in the grip of this frightful impotence that paralyses us in dreams; I try to cry out – I can't; I try to move – I can't; panting, with the most frantic effort, I try to turn round, to fling off this creature who is crushing and choking me – I can't do it.

And suddenly I wake up, terrified, drenched with sweat. I light a candle. I am alone.

After this crisis, which recurs every night, I fall at last into a quiet sleep until daybreak.

June 2. My condition has grown worse still. What can be the matter with me? Bromide is useless; douches are useless. Just now, by way of wearying a body already quite exhausted, I have gone for a tramp in the forest of Roumare. At first I thought that the fresh air, the clear, sweet air, full of the scents of grass and trees, was pouring new blood into my veins and new strength into my heart. I set off along a broad clearing, then turned towards Boville by a narrow route between two ranks of immensely tall trees that flung a thick, green roof, almost black, between the sky and me.

A sudden shudder ran through me, not a shudder of cold but a strange shudder of anguish.

I quickened my pace, uneasy at being alone in this wood – unreasonably, stupidly, terrified by the profound solitude. All at once

I felt that I was being followed, that someone was on my heels, quite close, near enough to touch me.

I swung round. I was alone. I saw behind me only the straight, open way I had come by, empty, high, terrifyingly empty; it stretched out ahead of me too, as far as the eye could see, empty and frightening.

I shut my eyes. Why? And I began to turn round on my heel at a great rate like a top. I almost fell; I opened my eyes again; the trees were dancing, the earth rocking; I was forced to sit. Then, ah! I didn't know now which way I had been walking. Strange thought! Strange! Strange thought! I knew nothing at all now. I took the right-hand way, and found myself back in the avenue that had led me into the middle of the forest.

June 3.   The night has been terrible. I am going to go away for several weeks. A short break will surely put me right.

July 2.   Home again. I am cured. I have had, moreover, a delightful holiday. I visited Mont-Saint-Michel, which I didn't know.

What a sight it is, arriving at Avranches as I did, towards dusk! The town lies on a slope and I was taken into the public garden on the edge of the town. A cry of astonishment broke from me. An immense bay stretched before me, as far as the eye could see, between opposite coasts that vanished in distant mist; and in the midst of this vast, yellow bay, under a gleaming, golden sky, a strange hill, sombre and peaked, thrust up out of the sands. The sun had just sunk, and on a horizon still riotous with colour was etched the outline of this fantastic rock that bore on its summit a fantastic monument.

At daybreak I went out to it. The tide was low as on the evening before, and as I drew near the miraculous abbey grew in height before my eyes. After several hours' walking I reached the monstrous pile of stones that supports the little city dominated by the great church. I clambered up the steep, narrow street, I entered the most wonderful

Gothic dwelling made for God on this earth, as vast as a town, with innumerable low rooms hunched under their ceilings, and lofty galleries supported by slender columns. I entered this gigantic granite jewel, as delicate as a piece of lace, adorned with towers and airy belfries where twisting stairways climb, towers that lift into the blue sky of day and the dark sky of night, strange heads bristling with gargoyles, devils, fantastic beasts and monstrous flowers, and are linked together by slender, carved arches.

When I stood on the top I said to the monk who accompanied me: 'What a glorious place you have here, Father!'

'We get strong winds,' he answered, and we fell into talk as we watched the incoming sea run over the sand and cover it as with a steel cuirass.

The monk told me stories, all the old stories of this place, legends, always legends.

One of them particularly impressed me. The people of the district, those who lived on the Mount, declared that at night they heard voices on the sands, followed by the bleating of two she-goats, one that called loudly and one softly. Unbelievers insisted that it was the mewing of sea birds which sometimes sound like bleatings, sometimes like human lamentations: but benighted fishermen swore that they had met an old shepherd wandering the dunes between two tides, below the little town cast off from the world. No one had ever seen the head, hidden by his cloak. He led a goat with the face of a man and a she-goat with the face of a woman, both with long white hair and speaking incessantly, arguing in an unknown tongue, then abruptly breaking off to bleat with all their force.

'Do you believe it?' I asked the monk.

He murmured, 'I don't know.'

'If,' I pursued, '– if there existed on the earth beings other than ourselves, why have we not long ago learned to know them? Why have you yourself not seen them? Why have I not seen them myself?'

He answered: 'Do we see the hundred-thousandth part of all that exists? Think, there's the wind, the greatest force in nature, which throws down men, shatters building, uproots trees, stirs up the sea into watery mountains, destroys cliffs and tosses the tall ships against the shore, the wind that kills, whistles, groans, roars – have you seen it, can you see it? Nevertheless, it exists.'

Before his simple reasoning I fell silent. This man was either a seer or a fool. I should not have cared to say which: I held my peace. What he had said I had often thought.

July 3. I slept badly; there must be a feverish influence at work here, for my coachman suffers from the same trouble as myself. Coming home yesterday, I noticed his strange pallor. 'What's the matter with you, Jean?' I demanded.

'I can't rest these days, sir. My nights eat into my days. I'm burning the candle at both ends. Since you went away, sir, there's been a spell on me.

The other servants are all right, however, yet I am terrified of it coming back.

July 4. It has surely got me again. My old nightmares have come back. Last night I felt someone crouching on me, his mouth on mine, drinking my life from between my lips. Yes, he sucked it from my throat like a leech. Then he rose from me, replete, and I awoke, so mangled, bruised, enfeebled, that I could not move. If this goes on for many days more, I shall certainly go away again.

July 5. Have I lost my reason? What happened last night is so strange that my head reels when I think of it.

I had locked my door as I do now every evening; then, feeling thirsty, I drank half a glass of water and I happened to notice that my carafe was full up right to its glass stopper.

I settled back after this and fell into one of my dreadful slumbers, out of which I was jerked about two hours later by a shock more frightful than any of the others.

Imagine a man murdered in his sleep, who wakes with a knife through his lung, with the death-rattle in his throat, covered with blood, unable to breathe, and on the point of death, understanding nothing – there you have it.

When I finally recovered my sanity, I was thirsty again; I lit a candle and went towards the table where I had placed my carafe. I lifted it and held it over my glass; not a drop ran out. It was empty! It was completely empty. At first, I simply didn't understand; then all at once a terrible sensation so overwhelmed me that I was forced to sit down, or rather, fell into a chair! Then I leaped up again and peered around me. Then I sat down again, lost in shock and fear, in front of the glass carafe. I gazed at it with a fixed stare, seeking an answer to the riddle. My hands were trembling. Had someone drunk the water? Who? I? It must have been me. Who could it have been but me? So I was a somnambulist, all unaware I was living the mysterious double life that raises the doubt whether there be not two selves in us, or whether, in moments when the spirit lies unconscious, an alien being, unknowable and unseen, inhabits the captive body that obeys this other as it obeys us, more readily that it obeys us.

Ah, who can grasp my frightful agony? Who can understand the feelings of a sane-minded, educated, thoroughly rational man, staring in abject terror through the glass of his carafe where the water has disappeared while he slept? I remained there until daylight, not daring to go back to bed.

July 6.　　　　　I am going mad. My carafe was emptied again last night – or rather, I emptied it.

Yet is it I? Is it I? Who can it be? Who? Oh, my God! Am I going mad? Who will save me?

July 10.   I have just had an astonishing proof. Listen to this!

On the 6th of July, before lying down in bed, I placed on my table wine, milk, water, bread and strawberries.

Someone drank – I drank – all the water, and a little of the milk. Neither the wine, nor the bread, nor the strawberries were touched.

On the 7th of July, I made the same experiment and got the same result.

On the 8th of July, I omitted the water and the milk. Nothing was touched.

Finally, on the 9th of July, I placed only the water and milk on my table, taking care to wrap the carafes in white muslin cloths and to tie down the stoppers. Then I rubbed my lips, my beard and my hands with a charcoal pencil and lay down.

The usual overpowering sleep seized me, followed shortly by the frightful wakening. I had not moved, My bedclothes themselves bore no marks. I rushed towards my table. The cloths wrapped round the bottles remained spotless. I untied the cords, shaking with fear. All the water had been drunk! All the milk had been drunk! Oh, my God! …

I am leaving for Paris at once.

July 13.   Paris. I suppose I must have lost my senses during the last few days. I must have been the sport of my disordered imagination, unless I really am a somnambulist or have fallen under one of those authenticated but hitherto inexplicable influences that we call suggestibility. However that may be, my disorder came very near to lunacy, and twenty-four hours in Paris have been enough to restore my balance.

Yesterday, after doing some errands and paying some visits which breathed new life into my soul, I ended my evening at the Théâtre Français. They were presenting a play by the younger Dumas; and his alert, forceful intelligence completed my cure. There can be no doubt that loneliness is a hazard to active minds. We need round us men who think and talk. When we live alone for long periods, we people the void with phantoms.

I returned to the hotel in high spirits, walking along the boulevards. Amid the jostling of the crowd, I reflected ironically on my terrors, on my hallucinations of a week ago, when I had believed – yes, believed – that an invisible being inhabited my body. How weak and shaken and speedily thrown off kilter are our brains immediately they are confronted by a tiny incomprehensible fact!

Instead of concluding by simply saying: 'I do not understand, because the cause eludes me,' at once we imagine frightening mysteries and supernatural powers.

July 14. *Fête de la République.* I walked through the streets. The rockets and the flags filled me with a childish joy. At the same time, it is very silly to be happy on a set day by order of the government. The mob is an imbecile herd, sometimes stupidly patient, sometimes violently rebellious. You say to it: 'Enjoy yourself,' and it enjoys itself. You say to it: 'Go and fight your neighbour.' It goes to fight. You say to it: 'Vote for the Emperor.' It votes for the Emperor. Then you say to it: 'Vote for the Republic.' And it votes for the Republic.

Its rulers are deluded, yet instead of obeying men they obey principles, which can only be half-baked, sterile and false by the very fact that they are principles, which is to say ideas taken to be unarguable and immutable in a world where nothing is sure, since light and sound are both illusions.

July 16. Yesterday I saw things that have profoundly disturbed me.

I dined with my cousin, Mme Sablé, whose husband commands the 76th Light Horse at Limoges. At her house I met two young women, one of whom has married a doctor, Dr Parent, who devotes himself largely to nervous illnesses and the extraordinary discoveries that are the outcome of the recent experiments in hypnosis and suggestion.

He told us at length about the amazing results obtained by English scientists and by the doctors of the Nancy school.

The facts that he adduced struck me as so fantastic that I confessed myself utterly incredulous.

'We are,' he declared, 'on the point of discovering one of the most important secrets of Nature, I mean one of the most important secrets of this earth – for there are certainly others as important, out there in the stars. Since man began to think, since he learned to express and record his thoughts, he has felt himself close to a mystery impenetrable by his clumsy and imperfect sense. He has tried to supplement the impotence of his organic powers by the force of his intelligence. So long as this intelligence was still at a rudimentary stage, this haunting sense of invisible phenomena clothed itself in crudely terrifying forms. Thus are born popular theories of the supernatural, the legends of wandering spirits, fairies, gnomes, ghosts. I'll add that God-myth itself, since our conceptions of the artificer-creator, to whatever religion they belong, are really the most commonplace, the most unintelligent, the least acceptable products of the fear-clouded brain of human beings. Nothing is truer than that saying of Voltaire's: "God has made man in His image, but man has paid Him back in his own coin."

'But for a little over a century we have had glimpses of a new knowledge. Mesmer and others have set our feet on a fresh path, and specifically during the last four or five years we have really reached surprising conclusions.'

My cousin, as incredulous as I, smiled. Dr Parent said to her, 'Shall I try to put you to sleep, Madame?'

'Yes, do.'

She seated herself in an armchair, and he fixed her with a hypnotic stare. As for me, I felt suddenly uneasy: my heart thumped, my throat contacted. I saw Mme Sablé's eyes grow heavy, her mouth twitch, her bosom rise and fall with her quick breathing. Within ten minutes she was asleep.

'Go behind her,' said the doctor.

I seated myself behind her. He put a visiting card in her hands and told her: 'Here is a looking-glass: what can you see in it?'

'I see my cousin,' she answered.

'What is he doing?'

'He is twisting his moustache.'

'And now?'

'He is drawing a photograph from his pocket.'

'Whose photograph is it?'

'His own.'

She was right! This photograph had been sent me at my hotel only that very evening.

'What is he doing in the photograph?'

'He is standing, with his hat in his hand.'

Evidently she saw, in this card, this piece of white pasteboard, what she would have seen in a mirror.

The young woman, terrified, cried: 'Stop, stop, stop!'

But the doctor said authoritatively: 'You will get up tomorrow at eight o'clock. Then you will call on your cousin at his hotel and you will beg him to lend you five thousand francs your husband has told you to get and will ask for on his next leave.'

Then he woke her up.

On my way back to the hotel, I thought about this curious séance. I was assailed by doubts, not of the absolutely unimpeachable good faith of my cousin whom since our childhood I had looked upon as my sister, but of the possibility of trickery on the doctor's part. Had he concealed a looking-glass in his hand and held it before the slumbering young woman with his visiting card? Professional conjurers do things as singular as that.

I had reached the hotel by now and I went to bed.

This morning, about half-past eight, I was roused by my man, who said to me, 'Mme Sablé wishes to speak to you at once, sir.'

I got hurriedly into my clothes and had her shown in.

She seated herself, very agitated, her eyes downcast, and, without lifting her veil, said:'I have a great favour to ask you, my dear cousin.'

'What is it, my dear?'

'I hate to ask it of you, and yet I must. I am in absolute need of five thousand francs.'

'You?'

'Yes, I – or rather my husband, who has told me to get it.'

I was so astounded that I stammered as I answered her. I wondered whether she and Dr Parent were not actually making fun of me, whether it weren't a little comedy they had prepared beforehand and were acting very well.

But as I watched her closely my doubts vanished entirely. The whole affair was so distasteful to her that she was shaking with anguish, and I saw that her throat was quivering with sobs.

I knew that she was very rich. I pressed her: 'What! Do you mean to say that your husband can't call on five thousand francs! Come, think. Are you sure he told you to ask me for it?'

She hesitated for a few moments as if she were making a tremendous effort to search her memory. Then she answered, 'Yes … yes … I'm quite sure.'

'Has he written to you?'

She hesitated again, reflecting. I guessed at the tortured striving of her mind. She didn't know. She only knew that she had to borrow five thousand francs from me for her husband. Then she risked a lie.

'Yes, he has written to me.'

'But when? You didn't speak to me about it yesterday.'

'I got his letter this morning.'

'Can you let me see it?'

'No … no … no … it is very intimate … too personal … I've … I've burned it.'

'Your husband must be in debt, then.'

Again she hesitated, then answered:

'I don't know.'

I told her abruptly: 'The fact is I can't lay my hands on five thousand francs at the moment, my dear.'

A kind of agonised wail broke from her.

'O, I implore you, I implore you, get it for me.'

She grew dreadfully excited, clasping her hands as if she were praying to me. The tone of her voice changed as I listened: she wept, stammering with grief, goaded by the irresistible command that had been laid on her.

'Oh, I implore you to get it … If you knew how unhappy I am! … I must have it today.'

I took pity on her.

'You shall have it at once, I promise you,'

'Thank you, thank you,' she cried. 'How kind you are!'

'Do you remember,' I went on, 'what happened at your house yesterday evening?'

'Yes.'

'Do you remember that Dr Parent put you to sleep?'

'Yes.'

'Very well, he ordered you to come this morning and borrow five thousand francs from me, and you are now obeying the suggestion.'

She considered this for a moment and answered:

'Because my husband wants it.'

I spent an hour trying to convince her, but I could not do so.

When she left, I ran across to the doctor's house. He was just going out, and he listened to me with a smile. Then he said, 'Now do you believe?'

'I cannot but.'

'Let's go and call on your cousin.'

She was already asleep on a day-bed, overwhelmed with weariness. The doctor felt her pulse, and looked at her for some time, one hand lifted towards her eyes, that slowly closed under the irresistible compulsion of his magnetic influence.

As she slept, he spoke to her. 'Your husband has no further need for five thousand francs. You will forget that you begged your cousin to lend it to you, and if he speaks to you about it, you will not understand.'

Then he woke her up. I drew a wallet from my pocket.

'Here is what you asked me for this morning, my dear.'

She was so dumbfounded that I dared not press the matter. I did, however, try to rouse her memory, but she denied it fiercely, thought I was making fun of her and at last was almost angry.

Back at the hotel. The experiment has disturbed me so profoundly that I could not each lunch.

July 19.   I have told several people about this adventure and been laughed at for my pains. I don't know what to thing now. The wise man says: *Perhaps?*

July 21.   I dined at Bougival, then I spent the evening at the rowing club dance. There's no doubt that everything is a question of places and people. To believe in the supernatural in the island of Grenouillère would be the height of folly ... but at the top of Mont-Saint-Michel? ... in the Indies? We are frightfully influenced by our surroundings. I am going home next week.

July 30.   I have been home since yesterday. All is well.

August 2.   Nothing fresh. The weather has been glorious. I spend my days watching the Seine run past.

August 4.   The servants are quarrelling among themselves. They declare that someone breaks the glasses in the cupboard at night. My man blames the cook, who blames the houseman, who blames the other two. Who is the culprit? It would take a mighty clever man to find out.

August 6.   This time, I am not mad. I've seen ... I've seen ... I've seen ... I can doubt no more ... I've seen ... I'm still cold to my bones ... still terrified to the marrow ... I've seen! ...

At two o'clock, in broad daylight, I was walking in my rose garden ... between the autumn roses, that are just coming out.

As I paused to look at a *Géant des Batailles*, which bore three superb blooms, I saw, distinctly saw, right under my eyes, the stem of one of these roses bend as if an invisible hand had twisted it, then break as if the hand had plucked it. Then the flower described a curve in the air which an arm would have made carrying it towards a mouth, and it hung suspended in the clear air, just on its own, motionless, a terrifying scarlet splash three paces from my eyes.

I lost my head and flung myself on it, grasping at it. My fingers closed on nothing: it had disappeared. Then I was filled with a savage rage against myself: a rational, serious-minded man simply does not have such hallucinations.

Yet was it really an hallucination? I turned round to look for the bloom and found it immediately beneath the bush, broken off and lying between the two roses that still remained on the stem.

I went back to the house, my senses reeling. For I am sure now, sure as I am that day follows night, that there lives at my side an invisible being who feeds on milk and water, who can touch things, take hold of them move them from one place to another, is endowed therefore with a material nature, though imperceptible to our senses, and lives as I do, under my roof ...

August 7. I slept quietly. He has drunk the water from my carafe, but he did not disturb my sleep.

I wonder if I am mad. Sometimes as I walk in the blazing sunshine along the riverbank, I am filled with doubts of my sanity, not the vague doubts I have been feeling, but precise and uncompromising doubts. I have seen madmen; I have known men who were intelligent, lucid, even markedly clear-headed in everything in life except on one point. They talked quite clearly, easily and profoundly about everything, until suddenly their mind ran onto the rocks of their madness and was there rent in pieces, strewn to the winds and foundered in the fearful raging sea, filled with surging waves, fogs, squalls, such as we call 'insanity'.

I should certainly think myself mad, absolutely mad, if I were not conscious, if I were not perfectly aware of my state of mind, if I did not plumb and analyse it with such complete clearness. I can then be no worse than a sane man troubled with hallucinations. There must be some unknown disturbances that modern physiologists are trying to observe and elucidate; and this disturbance has opened a deep gulf in my mind, in the orderly and logical working of my thoughts. Similar phenomena take place in dreams that drag us through the most unreal phantasmagoria without surprising us, because the mechanism of judgment, the controlling censor, is asleep, while the imaginative faculty wakes and works. Can some part of the matrix that controls my mental keyboard have jammed?

Sometimes, after an accident, a man loses his power to remember proper names, or verbs, or figures, or simply dates. The localisation of all the various faculties of mind is now proven. Is there anything surprising, therefore, in the notion that my power of examining the unreality of certain hallucinations has ceased to function in my brain just now?

I thought of all this as I walked by the side of the water. The sunlight flung a mantle of light across the river, clothing the earth with beauty, filing my thoughts with love of life, of the swallows whose swift flight is a joy to my eyes, of the riverside grasses whose whisper soothes my ears.

Little by little, however, I fell prey to an inexplicable uneasiness. I felt as though some force, an occult force, were paralysing my movements, halting me, preventing me from going on, calling me back. I felt such a disturbing impulse to turn back as one feels when a beloved person has been left at home ill and one is possessed by a foreboding that the illness has taken a turn for the worse.

So, in spite of myself, I did turn back, sure that I should find bad news waiting in my house, a letter or a telegram. There was nothing; and I was left more surprised and uneasy than if I had had yet another fantastic vision.

August 8.　　　Yesterday I endured a frightful night. He did not manifest himself again, but I feel him near me, spying on me, watching me, penetrating me, dominating me, more to be feared when he hides himself thus than if he gave notice of his constant, invisible presence by supernatural phenomena.

However, I slept.

August 9.　　　Nothing, but I am afraid.

August 10.　　　Nothing; what will happen tomorrow?

August 11.　　　Still nothing: I can't remain in my home any longer, with this fear and these thoughts in my mind: I shall go away.

August 12.　　　Ten o'clock in the evening. I have been wanting to go away all day. I can't. I have been wanting to carry out the easy, simple act that will set me free – just go out – get into my carriage to go to Rouen – I can't. Why?

August 13.   Under the affliction of certain maladies, all the resources of one's physical being seem crushed, all one's energy exhausted, one's muscles flaccid, one's bones grown as soft as flesh and one's flesh turned to water. In a strange and wretched fashion I suffer all these pains in my spiritual being. I have no strength, no courage, no control over myself, no power even to summon my will. I can no longer will; yet someone wills for me – and I obey.

August 14.   I am lost. Someone has taken possession of my soul and is master of it; someone orders all my acts, all my movements, all my thoughts. I am no longer anything in myself, I am only a spectator, enslaved, and terrified by all the things I do. I wish to go out. I cannot. He does not wish it; so I remain, dazed, trembling, in the armchair where he keeps me seated. I desire no more than to get up, to raise myself, so that I can think I am master of myself again. I can't do it. I am riveted to my seat; and my seat is fast to the ground in such fashion that no force could lift us.

Then, all at once, I must, must, go to the bottom of my garden and pick strawberries and eat them. Oh, my God! My God! My God! Is there a God? If there is one, deliver me, save me, help me! Pardon me! Pity me! Have mercy on me! How I suffer! How I am tortured! How terrible this is!

August 15.   Think how my poor cousin was possessed and overmastered when she came to borrow five thousand francs from me. She submitted to an alien will that had entered into her, as if it were another soul, a parasitic, tyrannical soul. Is the world coming to an end?

But what is this being, this invisible being who is ruling me? This unknowable creature, this rover from a supernatural race.

So Unseen Ones exist? Then why is it that since the world began they have never manifested themselves unmistakably, as they do now?

I have never read of anything like the things that are happening under my roof. If I could only leave it, if I could go away, fly far away and return no more, I should be saved, but I can't.

August 16. Today I was able to escape for two hours, like a prisoner who finds the door of his cell accidentally left open. I felt I was suddenly set free, that he had withdrawn himself. I ordered the horses to be put to the carriage as quickly as possible and I reached Rouen. Oh, what a joy it was to find myself able to tell a man, 'Drive to Rouen' and be obeyed!

I stopped at the library and I asked them to lend me the long treatise of Dr Hermann Herestauss on the unseen inhabitants of the antique and modern worlds.

Then, just as I was getting back into my carriage with the words, 'To the station,' on my lips, I shouted – I didn't speak, I shouted – in a voice so loud that the passers-by turned round: 'Home,' and I fell, overwhelmed with misery, onto the cushions of my carriage. He had found me again and taken possession once more.

August 17. What a night! What a night! Even so it seems to me I ought to congratulate myself. I read until one o'clock in the morning. Hermann Herestauss, a doctor of philosophy and theogony, has written an account of all the invisible beings who wander among men or have been conjured by men's minds. He describes their origins, their domains, their power. Yet none of them is the least like the being who haunts me. It is as if even since man became capable of thought he has had a menacing presentiment of some new being, mightier than himself who shall succeed him in this world. And in his terror, sensing him drawing near and unable to guess at the nature of this master, he has created a whole host of occult beings, dim phantoms born of fear.

Well, I read until one o'clock and then I seated myself near my open window to cool my head and my thoughts in the gentle air of night.

It was fine and warm. In other times how should I have loved such a night!

No moon. The stars trembled and glittered in the black depths of the sky. Who dwells in these worlds? What forms of life, what living creatures, what animals or plants do they hold? The thinkers in those far-off universes – what more do they know than we? What more can they do that we? What do they see that we do not know of? Perhaps one of them, some day or other, will cross the gulf of space and appear on our earth to conquer it, just as in olden days the Normans crossed the sea to subdue weaker nations.

We are so infirm, so defenceless, so ignorant, so small, on this grain of dust that revolves and crumbles in a drop of water. So musing, I fell asleep, in the fresh evening air.

I slept for about forty minutes and opened my eyes again without moving, roused by I know not what vague and weird emotions. At first I saw nothing, then all at once I thought that the page of a book lying open on my table had turned over of itself. Not a breath of air came in at the window. I was surprised and I sat waiting. About four minutes later, I saw, I saw, yes, I saw with my own eyes another page come up and turn back on the preceding one, as if a finger had folded it back. My armchair was empty, seemed empty; but I realised that he was there, he, sitting in my place and reading. In one wild spring, like a maddened beast springing on his trainer, I crossed the room to seize him, crush him, kill him. But before I had reached it my seat turned right over as if he had fled before me … my table rocked, my lamp fell and was extinguished, and my window slammed shut as if I had surprised a malefactor who had hurled himself out into the night, slamming it shut behind him, tugging at the sashes with all his force.

So he had run away; he had been afraid, afraid of me, me!

In that case – in that case, tomorrow … or the day after … or some day … I should be able to get him between my fingers, and crush him into the ground. Don't dogs sometimes bite and savage their masters' throats?

August 18.   I've been thinking things over all day. Oh, yes, I'll obey him, satisfy his impulses, do his will, make myself humble, submissive, servile. He is the stronger. But an hour will come …

August 19.   I know now – I know – I know all! I have just ready the following in the *Revue du Monde Scientifique*:

'A strange piece of news reaches us from Rio de Janerio. Madness, an epidemic of madness, comparable to the contagious outbursts of dementia that attacked the peoples of Europe in the Middle Ages, is raging at this day in the Province of San Paulo. The distracted in habitants are leaving their houses, deserting their villages, abandoning their fields, declaring themselves to be pursued, possessed and ordered about like a human herd by certain invisible but tangible beings, vampires of some kind who feed on their vitality while they sleep and also drink milk and water while not, apparently, touching any other form of food.

'Professor Don Pedro Henriquez, accompanied by several medical authorities, has set out for the Province of San Paulo to study on the spot the origins and manifestations of this surprising madness, and to suggest to the Emperor such measures as appear to him most likely to restore the delirious inhabitants to sanity.'

Ah! I remember, I remember the lovely Brazilian three-master that sailed past my windows on the 8th of last May, on her way up the Seine. I thought her such a bonny, white, attractive craft. The Being was on board her, come from over the sea, where his race is born. He saw me. He saw my house, while like the ship, and he jumped from the vessel to the bank. Oh, my God!

Now I know, I understand. The reign of man is at an end.

He is here, he whom the primal fears of early man taught them to dread. He who was exorcised by troubled priests, and evoked at dead of night by sorcerers who never actually saw him materialise, to whom the presentiments of the temporary master of this world lent all the monstrous or beguiling forms of gnomes, spirits, jinns, fairies and hobgoblins. Primitive terror visualised him in the crudest forms; later wiser men have seen him more clearly. Mesmer foresaw him, and it is ten years since doctors made a precise investigation into the nature of his power, even before he himself exercised it. They have been making a plaything of this weapon of the new God, this imposition of a mysterious will on the enslaved soul of man. They called it magnestism, hypnosis, suggestibility – what you will. I have seen them amusing themselves with this dreadful power like foolish children. Woe to us! Woe to man! He is here – the – the – what is his name? The … it seems as if he were shouting his name in my year, yet I cannot hear it … the … yes … he is shouting it … I'm listening … I can't hear … again, say it again … the … Horla … I heard … the Horla … It's him. The Horla … He has come!

Ah, the vulture ate the dove, the wolf ate the lamb; the lion devoured the sharp-horned buffalo; man slew the lion with arrow, spear and gun; but the Horla is going to make of man what we have made of the horse and the cow: his chattel, his servant, his food, by the mere force of his will. Woe upon us!

Yet sometimes the beast turns on his master and kills him. I too want … I could … but I must know him, touch him, see him. Scientists say that the eye of the beast is not like our own and does not see as ours does … and my eye fails to show me this newcomer who is oppressing me.

Why? Oh, the words of the monk of Mont-Saint-Michel come to my mind: 'Do we see the hundred-thousandth part of all that exists? Think, there's the wind, the greatest force in Nature, which throws down men, shatters buildings, uproots trees, whips up the sea into watery mountains, destroys cliffs and tosses the tall ships against the shore, the wind that kills, whistles, groans, roars – have you seen it, can you see it? Nevertheless, it exists.'

And I considered further: my eye is so weak, so imperfect, that it does not distinguish even solid bodies if they are transparent as glass is. If a looking-glass that has no foil backing bars my path, I hurl myself against it as a bird that has got into a room breaks its head on the window-pane. How many other things deceive and mislead my eye? What is there surprising in its failure to see a new body that offers no resistance to the passage of light?

A new being! why not? He must assuredly come! Why should we be the last? Why is he not seen by our eyes as are all the beings created before us? Because his nature is nearer perfection, hi body finer and completer than ours – ours, which is so weak, so clumsily conceived, encumbered by organs always tired, always under strain like a too complex mechanism, which lives like a vegetable or a beast, drawing its substance painfully from the air, herbs and flesh, an animal subject to sickness, deformity and corruption, drawing its breath in pain, ill-regulated, simple and eccentric, ingeniously ill-made, clumsily and delicately put together, a kind of rough sketch of a being who might become intelligent and noble.

There have been so few of us in the world, from the oyster to Man. Why not one more, when we reach the end of the period of time that separates each successive appearance of a species from that which appeared before it?

Why not one more? Why not also new kinds of trees bearing monstrous flowers, blazing with colour and filling all the countryside with their scent? Why not other elements than fire, air, earth and water? There are four, only four sources of our being! How paltry! Why not forty, four hundred, four thousand? How poor, niggardly and brutish is life! – grudgingly given, meanly conceived, stupidly executed. Consider the grace of the elephant, the hippopotamus! The elegance of the camel!

You bid me consider the butterfly! – a winged flower! I can imagine one as vast as a hundred worlds, with wings for whose shape, beauty, colour and sweep I can find no words. Yet I see it … it goes from star to star, refreshing and perfuming them with the soft, gracious wind of its passing. And the people of the upper air watch it pass in an ecstasy of joy!

What is the matter with me? It is he, he, the Horla, who is haunting me, filing my head with these absurdities! H is in me, he has become my soul; I will kill him!

August 19.   I will kill him. I have seen him! I was sitting at my table yesterday evening, pretending to be absorbed in writing. I knew well that he would come and prowl round me, very close to me, so close that I might be able to touch him, seize him, perhaps? And then! … then, I would be filled with the strength of desperation; I would have hands, knees, chest, face, teeth to strangle him, crush him, tear him, rend him.

With every sense quiveringly alert, I watched for him.

I had lit both my lamps and the eight candles on my chimneypiece, as if I thought I should be more likely to discover him by this bright light.

Opposite me was my bed, an old oak fore-poster; on my right, the fireplace; on my left, my door carefully shut after I had left it open for a long time to attract him. Behind me, a very tall wardrobe with a mirror front, which I used every day to shave and dress by, and in which I always looked at myself from head to foot whenever I passed in front of it.

Well, to deceive him, I pretended to write, because he was spying on me too; and, all at once, I felt, I was certain, that he was reading over my shoulder, that he was there, his breath on my ear.

I stood up, my hand outstretched, and turned round, so quickly that I almost fell. What do you think? … the room was as light as day, and

I could not see myself in my looking-glass! It was empty, clear, deep, filled with light! I was not reflected in it ... and I was standing in front of it. I could see the wide limpid expanse of glass from top to bottom. I stared at it with a distraught gaze: I dared not step forward, I dared not move; nevertheless I felt that he was there, he whose immaterial body had swallowed up my reflection, but he would elude me still.

How frightened I was! A moment later my reflection began to appear in the depths of the looking-glass, in a sort of mist, as if I were looking at it though water. This water seemed to flow from left to right, slowly, so that moment by moment my reflection emerged more distinctly. It was like the passing of an eclipse. The thing that was concealing me appeared to possess no sharply defined outlines, but a kind of transparent opacity that gradually cleared.

At last I could see myself from head to foot, just as I would see myself every day when I looked in the glass.

I had seen him! The horror if it is still on my, making me shudder.

August 20.　　　Kill him – but how, since I cannot touch him? Poison? But he would see me put it in the water; and besides, would our poisons affect an immaterial body? No ... no, they certainly would not ... Then how? – how?

August 21.　　　I have sent for a locksmith from Rouen, and ordered him to fit my room with iron shutters, such as they have in certain hotels in Paris, to keep out robbers. He is to make me, also, an iron door as well. Everyone thinks me a cowards, but much I care about that!

September 10.　　Rouen, Hôtel Continental. It is done ... it is done ...but is he dead? My brain reels with that I have seen.

Yesterday the locksmith put up my iron shutters and my iron door, and I left everything open until midnight, although it began to get cold.

All at once I felt his presence, and I was filled with joy, a mad joy. I rose slowly to my feet, and walked about the room for a long time, so that he should suspect nothing; then I took off my boots and carelessly drew on my slippers. Then I closed my iron shutters, and, sauntering back towards the door, I double-locked it too. Then I walked back to the window and secured it with a padlock, putting the key in my pocket.

Suddenly I realised that he was prowling round me anxiously. He was afraid now, and commanding me to open them for him. I almost yielded. I did not yield but, leaning on the door, I set it ajar, just wide enough for me to slip out backwards; and as I am very tall my head touched the lintel. I am sure that he could not have got out and I shut him in, alone, all alone. What joy! I had him! Then I ran downstairs: in the drawing-room which is under my room, I took both my lamps and emptied the oil all over the carpet and the furniture, everything; then I set it on fire and, having double-locked the main door, fled!

I went and hid myself at the bottom of my garden, in a grove of laurels. How long it took, how long! Everything was dark, silent, still; not a breath of air, not a star, mountains of unseen clouds that lay heavily, how heavily, on my spirit.

I kept my gaze fixed on my house and waited. How long it took! I was beginning to think that the fire had died out of itself, or that he, He, had put it out, when one of the lower windows fell in under the fierce breath of the fire and a flame, a great red and yellow flame, a long curling, caressing flame, leaped up the white wall and pressed its kiss on the roof itself. A flood of light flowed over trees, branches, leaves, and with that a shudder, a shudder of fear, ran through them. The birds woke; a dog howled: I thought the dawn was at hand. In a moment two more windows burst into flame and I saw that the lower half of my house was now one frightful furnace. But a cry, a frightful, piercing, agonised cry, a woman's cry, stabbed the night, and two skylights opened. I had forgotten my servants. I saw their distraught faces and their wildly waving arms...

Frantic with horror, I began to run towards the village, shouting: 'Help! Help! Fire! Fire!' I met people already on their way to the house and I turned back with them to look at it.

By now the house was no more than a horrible and magnificent funeral pyre, a monstrous pyre lighting up the whole earth, a pyre that was consuming men, and consuming Him, Him, my prisoner, the new Being, the new Master, the Horla!

Suddenly the entire roof fell in with a crash, and a volcano of flames leaped to the sky. Through all the windows open on the furnace, I saw the fiery vat, and I reflected that he was there, in this oven dead …

Dead? Perhaps. – His body? Perhaps that body through which light passed could not be destroyed by the methods that kill our bodies.

Suppose he were not dead? … Maybe only time has power over the Invisible and Dreadful One. Why should this transparent, unknowable body, this body of the spirit, fear sickness, injury, infirmity, premature destruction?

Premature destruction? The source of all human dread! After man, the Horla. After him who can die any day, any hour, any moment, by accidents of all kinds, comes he who can die only at his appointed day, hour and moment, when he has attained the limit of his existence.

No … no … beyond doubt – he is not dead. So … so … I must kill myself! …

TWO LITTLE SOLDIERS

Every Sunday, as soon as they were free, the little soldiers would go for a walk. On leaving the barracks, they turned right, crossed Courbevoie with rapid strides, as though on a forced march; then, as the houses grew scarcer, they slowed down to follow the dusty road that leads to Bezons.

They were small and thin, lost in their ill-fitting capes, too large for them and too long, the sleeves covering their hands and their red trousers falling in folds around their ankles. Under the high, stiff shakos one could just barely make out two skinny Breton faces, with their calm, naïve blue eyes. They never spoke on their way, going straight ahead, the same idea in each one's mind taking the place of conversation. For at the entrance of the little forest of Champioux they had found a spot that reminded them of home, and they did not feel happy anywhere else.

At the crossing of the Colombes and Chatou roads, when they arrived under the trees, they would take off their heavy, oppressive headgear and wipe their foreheads.

They always paused for a while on the bridge at Bezons to look at the Seine. They stood there several minutes, leaning over the railing, to gaze at the white sails, which perhaps reminded them of their home and at the fishing smacks leaving for open water.

As soon as they had crossed the Seine, they would purchase provisions at the baker's and the wine merchant's. Two pennyworth of bread and a quart of wine made up luncheon which they carried wrapped up in their handkerchiefs. Only when they were out of the village would their gait slacken and they would begin to talk.

Before them was a stretch of land with a few clumps of trees which led to woodland, a little forest which seemed to remind them of that other forest at Kermarivan. Wheat and oat fields bordered the narrow path. Each time Jean Kerderen said to Luc Le Ganidec:

'It's just like home, just like Plounivon.'

'Yes, it's just like home.'

And on they went, side by side, their minds full of misty memories of home. They saw the fields, the hedges, the forests and the shore.

Every time they stopped near a large stone on the edge of a private estate, because it reminded them of the dolmen of Locneuven.

As soon as they reached the first clump of trees, Luc Le Ganidec would cut off a small stick, and whittling it slowly, would stroll on, thinking of his people at home. Jean Kerderen carried the provisions.

From time to time, Luc would mention a name, or allude to some boyish prank which would give them food for plenty of thought. So the home country, dear and distant, would little by little gain possession of their minds, sending them back through space to familiar sights and sounds, the familiar scenery, with the fragrance of its green fields and sea air. They were no longer aware of the smells of the city. And in their ruminations they saw their friends setting out, perhaps forever, for the dangerous fishing grounds.

They were walking slowly, Luc Le Ganidec and Jean Kerderen, contented and sad, haunted by a sweet sorrow, the slow and penetrating sorrow of a captive animal which recalls the days of its freedom.

And when Luc had finished whittling his stick, they came to a little nook where every Sunday they took their meal. They found the two bricks which they had hidden in a hedge and made a little fire of dry branches to roast their sausages on the end of their knives.

When their last crumb of bread had been eaten and the last drop of wine had been drunk, they stretched themselves out on the grass side by side, without speaking, their half-closed eyes with a faraway look, their hands clasped as in prayer, their red-trousered legs mingling with the bright colours of the wild flowers.

Towards noon they glanced, from time to time, towards the village of Bezons, for the dairymaid would soon be coming. Every Sunday she would pass in front of them on the way to milk her cow, the only cow in the neighbourhood which was sent out to pasture.

Soon they would see the girl coming through the fields, and it pleased them to watch the sparkling sunbeams reflected from her shining pail. They never spoke of her. They were just glad to see her, without understanding why.

She was a tall strapping girl, freckled and tanned by the open air – a girl typical of the Parisian suburbs.

Once, on noticing that they were always sitting in the same place, she said to them: 'Do you always come here?'

Luc Le Ganidec, more daring than his friend stammered: 'Yes, we come here on our time off.'

That was all. But the following Sunday, on seeing them, she smiled with the kindly smile of a woman who understood their shyness, and she asked: 'What are you doing here? Are you watching the grass grow?'

Luc, cheered. 'Maybe,' he smiled.

'It's not growing fast, is it?'

He answered, still laughing: 'Not exactly.'

She continued on her way. But when she came back with a pail full of milk, she stopped before them and said: 'Want some? It'll remind you of home.'

Perhaps instinctively, she had guessed and touched the right spot.

Both were moved. Then, not without difficulty, she poured some milk into the bottle in which they had brought their wine. Luc started to drink, making sure he didn't take more than his share. Then he passed the bottle to Jean. She stood before them hands on hips, her pail at her feet, enjoying the pleasure she was giving them. Then off she went saying: 'Well, goodbye til next Sunday.'

For a long time they watched her tall form as it receded in the distance, blending with the background, and finally disappeared.

The following week, as they left the barracks, Jean said to Luc: 'Don't you think we ought to buy her something?'

They were sorely challenged by the task of choosing something to bring the dairymaid. Luc was in favour of bringing her some chitterlings, but Jean, who had a sweet tooth, thought confectionery would be the best thing. He won, and so they went to a grocery to buy two sous' worth of red and white sweets.

This time they ate more quickly than usual, spurred by anticipation.

Jean was the first one to notice her. 'There she is', he said; and Luc answered: 'Yes, there she is.'

She smiled when she saw them and cried: 'Well, how are you today?'

They both answered together, 'All right! How's everything with you?'

Then she started to talk of simple things which might interest them, of the weather, of the crops, her masters. They didn't dare to offer their sweets, which were slowly melting in Jean's pocket. Finally, Luc, growing bolder, murmured: 'We've brought you something.'

She asked: 'Let's see it.'

Then Jean, blushing to the tips of his ears, reached in his pocket and drawing out the little paper bag, handed it to her.

She began to eat the sweets. The two soldiers sat in front of her, moved and delighted.

At last she went to do her milking, and when she came back she again gave them some milk.

They thought of her all through the week and often spoke of her. The following Sunday she settled beside them for a longer time.

The three of them sat there, side by side, their eyes looking far away into the distance, their hands clasped over their knees, and they told each other little incidents and little details of the villages where they were born, while the cow, waiting to be milked, stretched her heavy head towards the girl and mooed.

Soon the girl consented to eat with them, and to take a sip of wine. Often she brought them plums in her pocket, for plums were now ripe. Her presence enlivened the little Breton soldiers, who chattered away like two birds.

One Tuesday something unusual happened to Luc Le Ganidec: he asked for leave and did not return until ten o'clock at night. Jean worried and racked his brain to account for his friend having obtained leave.

The following Friday, Luc borrowed ten sous from one of his friends, and once more asked and obtained leave for several hours.

When he started out with Jean on Sunday he seemed a bit strange, disturbed and somehow altered. Kerderen did not understand, he vaguely suspected something, but had no means of telling what it might be.

They went straight to the usual place, and lunched slowly. Neither was hungry.

Soon the girl appeared. They watched her approach as they always did. When she was near, Luc arose and went towards her. She put down her pail on the ground and kissed him. She kissed him passionately, throwing her arms around his neck, without paying attention to Jean, without even noticing that he was there.

Poor Jean was dazed, so dazed that he could not understand. His mind was in confusion and his heart was broken without so much as realising why.

Then the girl sat down beside Luc and they started to chat.

Jean was not looking at them. He understood now why his friend had gone out twice during the week. He felt the pain and the sting which treachery and deceit leave in their wake.

Luc and the girl went together to attend to the cow.

Jean followed them with his eyes. He saw them disappear side by side, the red trousers of his friend making a scarlet spot against the white road. It was Luc who fixed the stake to which the cow was tethered. The girl stooped down to milk the cow, while he absentmindedly stroked the animal's glossy neck. Then they left the pail in the grass and disappeared into the woods.

Jean could no longer see anything but the wall of leaves through which they had passed. He was so unmanned that he did not have strength to stand. He stayed there, motionless, bewildered and grieving - filled with simple passionate grief. He wanted to weep, to run away, to hide somewhere, never to see anyone again.

Then he saw them coming back again. They were walking slowly, hand in hand, as village lovers do. Luc was carrying the pail.

After kissing him again, the girl went on, with a nonchalant nod to Jean. She didn't offer him any milk that day.

The two little soldiers sat side by side, motionless as always, silent and quiet, their calm faces in no way betraying the trouble in their hearts. The sun shone down on them. From time to time they could hear the plaintive lowing of the cow. At the usual time, they arose to return.

Luc was whittling a stick. Jean carried the empty bottle. He left it at the wine merchant's in Bezons. Then they stopped on the bridge, as they did every Sunday, and watched the water flowing by.

Jean leaned over the railing, farther and farther, as though he had seen something in the stream that hypnotized him. Luc said to him: 'What's the matter? Do you want a drink?'

He had hardly said the last work when Jean's head carried away the rest of his body and the little blue and red soldier fell like a canonball and disappeared in the water.

Paralysed with horror, Luc tried vainly to shout for help. In the distance downriver he saw something move: then his friend's head bobbed up out of the water only to disappear again. Farther down he again caught sight of a hand, just one hand, which appeared and again disappeared. Nothing more.

The boatmen who had rushed to the scene found no body that day.

Luc ran back to the barracks, crazed, and with eyes and voice full of tears, told what had happened. 'He leaned – he was leaning – so far over – that his head carried him away – and – he – fell – he – fell –'

Emotion choked him. He could say no more. If only he had known…

THE CHRISTENING

'Well, doctor, a little brandy?'
'With pleasure.'

The old ship's surgeon, holding out his glass, watched it as it slowly filled with the golden liquid. Then, holding it in front of his eyes, he let the light from the lamp stream through it, breathed in its fragrance, sampled a few drops and smacked his lips with relish. Then he said:

'Ah the divine poison! Or rather, the seductive murderer, the adorable destroying angel!'

'You people don't know it the way I do. You may have read that admirable book entitled "L'Assommoir", but you haven't seen as I have, alcohol exterminate a whole tribe of savages, a little kingdom of negroes, drink – calmly unloaded by the barrel by red-bearded English seamen.

'Right near here, in a little village in Brittany near Pont-l'Abbé, I once witnessed a strange and terrible tragedy caused by alcohol. I was spending my vacation in a little country house my father left me. You know that flat coast where the wind whistles day and night, where one sees, standing or stretched out, those giant rocks which in olden days were regarded as guardians, and which still have something majestic and awe-inspiring about them. I always expect to see them come to life and start tramping across the country with the slow and ponderous tread of giants, or to unfold enormous granite wings and fly toward Valhalla.

'All around is the sea, always ready on the slightest provocation to rise in its anger and shake its foamy mane at those bold enough to brave its wrath. And the men who ply this terrible sea, which with one gesture of its green back can overturn and swallow up their frail barks – they go out in the little boats, day and night, hardy, weary and drunk. They are often drunk. They've a saying which goes: "When the bottle is full you see the reef, but when it is empty you see it no more." Go into one of their houses; you will never find the father there, If you ask the woman what has become of her husband, she'll stretch her arms out towards the dark ocean which murmurs and roars along the coast. There he remained one night when he had had too much to drink; so did her eldest son. She's four more big strong fair-haired boys. Soon it'll be their turn.

'As I was saying, I was living in a little house near Pont-l'Abbé. I was there alone with my servant, an old sailor, and with a local family that took care of the place in my absence. There were three of them: two sisters and the fellow, who had married one of them, a fellow called Kerandec, who looked after the garden.

'Not long before Christmas my gardener's wife presented him with a boy. The husband asked me to stand as godfather. I could hardly turn aside the request, and he borrowed ten francs from me – for the cost of the christening, so he said.

'The second day of January was chosen as the date of the ceremony. For a week the earth had been draped with an enormous white carpet of snow, which made this flat, featureless country seem vast and limitless. The ocean seemed black in contrast with this white plain; one could see it rolling, raging and tossing its waves as though wishing to annihilate its pale neighbour, which appeared to be dead, being so calm, quiet and cold.

'At nine o'clock, the father, Kerandec, came to my door with his sister-in-law, the big Kermagan, and the nurse, who carried the infant wrapped up in a blanket. We set off for the church. The weather was so cold that it seemed to freeze the skin and crack it open. I was thinking of the poor little creature being carried on ahead of us, and I said to myself that this Breton race must surely be of iron, if their children were able, as soon as they were born, to stand such an outing.

'We got to the church, but the door was closed; the priest was late.

'Then the nurse sat down on one of the steps and began to undress the child. At first I thought there must have been some slight accident, but I saw that they were leaving the poor little fellow naked, completely naked in the icy air. Furious at such impudence, I protested: "Why, you are crazy! You will kill the child!"

'The woman answered quite placidly: "Oh no sir; he must come naked before le bon Dieu."

'Father and aunt looked on unperturbed. It was the custom. If it were not adhered to, misfortune was sure to attend the little one.

'I scolded, threatened and pleaded. I used force to try to cover the frail creature. All was in vain. The nurse ducked away from me through the snow, and the body of that wee scrap turned purple. I was about to leave these wretches when I saw the priest coming across the country, followed by the sexton and a young lad. I ran towards him and gave vent to my indignation. He showed no surprise nor did he quicken his pace in the least. He answered:

'"What can you expect, sir? It's the custom. They all do it and it's no good trying to stop them."

'"But at least hurry up!" I cried.

'He answered: "I can't go any faster."

'He went into the vestry, while we remained outside on the church steps. I was suffering. But what about the poor little creature who was howling from the effects of the biting cold!

'At last the door opened. We entered the church. But the poor child had to remain naked throughout the ceremony. It was interminable. The priest stammered over the Latin words and garbled them woefully. He moved slowly and with a ponderous tread. His white surplice chilled my heart. It seemed as though, in the name of a pitiless and barbarous god, he had wrapped himself in another species of snow to torture this little piece of humanity which endured so the cold.

'At last the christening was finished according to the rites and I saw the nurse once more take the frozen whimpering infant and wrap it in the blanket.

'The priest said to me: "Will you come and sign the register?"

'Turning to my gardener, I said: "Buck up and get back home quickly so that you can warm that child." I gave him some advice on how to ward off, if not too late, a bad attack of pneumonia. He promised to follow my instructions and left with his sister-in-law and the nurse. I followed the priest into the vestry, and when I had signed he demanded five francs for expenses.

'As I had already given the father ten francs, I refused to pay twice. The priest threatened to destroy the paper and annul the ceremony. I, in turn, threatened him with the district attorney. The dispute went on and on, but finally I paid the five francs.

'As soon as I reached home I went down to Kerandec's to find out if everything was all right. Neither father, nor sister-in-law, nor nurse had yet returned. The child's mother, who had remained alone and in bed, was shivering with cold and starving, for she had had nothing to eat since the day before.

"Where the deuce can they have gone?" I asked. She answered without surprise or anger, "They'll have gone off for a drink to celebrate." It was the custom. Then I thought of my ten francs intended for the church service, which were now doubtless paying for the booze.

'I sent in some broth to the mother and ordered a good fire to be lit in the room. I was upset and angry and promised myself to let these yokels have it from the shoulder wondering what ghastliness was going to befall the poor brat.

'It was already six, and they still hadn't returned, I told my servant to wait up for them and went to bed. I soon fell asleep and slept like a top. At daybreak I was awakened by my servant, who was bringing me my hot water.

'As soon as my eyes were open I asked: "How about Kerandec?"

'The man hesitated. Then he stammered: "Oh! He came back all right, after midnight, and so drunk that he couldn't walk, and so were Kermagan and the nurse. I can only think they must have slept in a ditch, for the little one died and they never even noticed it."

'I jumped up out of bed crying: "What! The child is dead?"

'"Yes, sir. They brought it back to Mother Kerandec. When she saw it she began to cry, and now they are making her drink to console her."

'"What're you telling me? They're making her drink?"

'"Yes, sir. I only found it out this morning. Kerandec had no more brandy or money, so he took some wood alcohol which monsieur gave him for the lamp, and all four of them are now drinking that. The mother is feeling pretty sick right now."

'I had thrown on some clothes, and seizing a stick, with the intention of applying it to the backs of these brutes, I hurried towards the gardener's house.

'The mother was raving drunk beside the blue body of her dead baby. Kerandec, the nurse and the Kermagan woman were snoring on the floor. I had to take care of the mother who died towards noon.'

The old doctor was silent. He took up the brandy-bottle and poured out another glass. He held it up to the lamp, and the light streaming through it imparted to the liquid the amber colour of molten topaz. With one gulp he swallowed the treacherous gleaming liquid.